PROMISES, PROMISES

PROMISES, PROMISES

Paul & Louise
Kenneth

Kenneth Clare

Library of Congress Number: 2003093233
ISBN :   Hardcover   1-4134-0987-3
                Softcover   1-4134-0986-5

To order additional copies of this book, contact:
Xlibris Corporation
1-888-795-4274
www.Xlibris.com
Orders@Xlibris.com
18909

CONTENTS

With love and gratitude to my wife Anne

PREFACE

P*romises, Promises,* set in 16th century Europe, is, for the most part, a true account of a romance between Anna Trondson and James Hepburn. Anna was the seventeen-year-old, attractive daughter of a notable Norwegian sea-faring man and naval advisor to King Frederick II of Denmark and Norway. James Hepburn, The Lord High Admiral and 4th Earl of Bothwell in Scotland, was not only a dashing young naval officer of high rank but also an ambitious and aggressive political leader in Scotland. Anna met and fell in love with him in Copenhagen. Her intimate relationship with this prominent Scotsman is well known in Norway, and Norwegians even today refer to her as the "Skottefruen," a nickname which translates ambiguously as Scottish wife or simply as Scottish woman.

I came across these interesting individuals when researching my family history. In that research, I discovered the Trondson family which originated in the Hardanger area of western Norway. Kristoffer Trondson of this family, as noted, became a prominent naval figure. His daughter, Anna, also became a notable person but in quite a different way.

Trondson and his wife, Karen, members of the so-called "old nobility" of Norway, had a large family comprising seven daughters and one son. A Trondson daughter, Dorte, married Prince John Stuart, an illegitimate son of King James V of Scotland; John was a half brother of Mary Queen of Scots. Else, another of the seven sisters, married Anders Mowatt, a wealthy Scotsman and they settled in western Norway. Daughter Maren, was the wife of Olaf Jonsson Thieste, also an owner of a large estate in Norway. Kristine married a Norwegian landowner named Torbjorn Olavson Sandven. Magdalena married Erik Erikson Orm, and their son, like his grandfather, became a distinguished admiral in the Danish/ Norwegian navy. Margaret became the wife of a Danish nobleman named Jorgen Pedersson Stauer who served as a government administrator in western Norway. All of these daughters married "well."

Enno, the only son of Kristoffer Trondson and Karen, served in the armed forces of Denmark for a time. Later, he joined other armies and fought in several European wars. In 1567, he moved to Sweden where he became well acquainted with the royal family and, in particular, with King Eirik XIV and his brother, Duke Carl. Enno was named a Swedish nobleman. All apparently went well for him until a major theft was discovered in the Swedish royal household; Enno was a suspect and he suddenly left the country and settled in Germany. The following year, Enno killed a man and his wife and stole their possessions. As a result, he was apprehended, tried and hanged. The only son of Admiral Trondson must have been a great disappointment to his parents, who might have wished they had, instead, an eighth daughter.

Anna Trondson, the youngest of the seven sisters, was living with her parents in Copenhagen in 1560. In June of that year, the 25 year old Lord Admiral James Hepburn arrived for an official visit, coming as a representative of the Scottish Regent, Mary of Guise, to discuss naval matters with King Frederick and senior officers of the Danish navy, one of whom was Anna's father. Anna met the impressive Lord Admiral on his arrival and, during his visit of about three weeks, they became romantically involved. By the end of his stay, she was deeply in love with him. The lovers left Denmark together with plans to be married in Amsterdam. For a couple of weeks, they greatly enjoyed life in that attractive city. Over the years, Anna tenaciously sought to preserve a relationship that was often undermined by Bothwell's intense pursuit of high office in the government of Mary Queen of Scots and by the admiral's irresistible pursuit of other women.

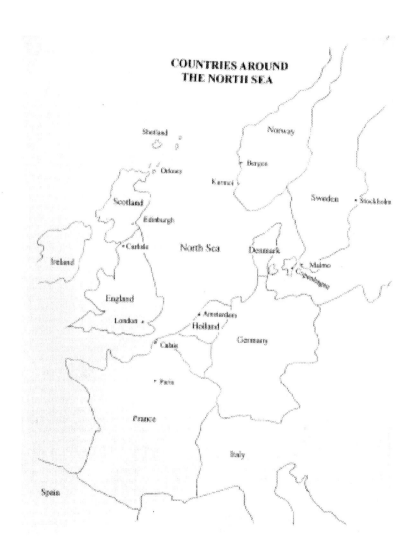

Countries Around the North Sea

CHAPTER 1

Anna Meets Admiral James Hepburn

in Copenhagen

"James has asked me to marry him and I have agreed." Anna told her parents. "I am thrilled. I love him so much." Before they could respond, she knew she must add the hard part. "We'll be married in Amsterdam,"

"I am not greatly surprised that you and James have decided to marry," her father remarked, "you two have been together so frequently during the past several weeks and seem very fond of each other." He did not comment on the place she said they were to be married.

"Oh darling, I am most happy for you," her mother replied, "but surely you want to be married here in Copenhagen, your home town, rather than in far-off Amsterdam. You must persuade James to have the marriage held here." Anna's mother, Karen Trondson, patted her daughter's knee reassuringly as they sat together in the living room. Anna's father let his wife speak for the two of them for the time being, although he had strong views on the subject.

"But, Mother, James must leave Copenhagen promptly and he insists that I accompany him aboard his ship." Anna knew that she must be firm or she might break down. Of course she wanted to marry in Copenhagen where her family and friends were, but James had to get back to Scotland, and she had to be with him. "I have already agreed to go with him," she continued, "and we will be married soon after our arrival in wonderful Amsterdam."

Anna's father, Admiral Kristoffer Trondson, could remain silent no longer.

"How could you just leave home in a sudden burst of excitement and travel to Holland with him as an unmarried woman? I have come to know your Scotsman quite well during his official visit here and he seems like a fine man. I am surprised he would ask you to do this. Please do as your mother suggests and plan to have the marriage in Copenhagen."

"I have already said that James must leave Copenhagen soon. Therefore there is no time to arrange a wedding here," Anna replied rising suddenly from her chair and throwing up her arms in exasperation.

"Let's all cool down and discuss the matter calmly," Karen stated quietly. "Don't you think, Anna, that you could persuade James to stay a few more days than planned so that we could arrange a local wedding. I will do everything I can to shorten the length of time for arrangements. You know your friends would be pleased to attend."

"Mother, you know from past experience with weddings that it would take one to two weeks. James cannot remain here that long."

All of them were quiet for a moment. Kristoffer and Karen Trondson knew they were up against a stubborn daughter. The old admiral tried one more time.

"Won't you at least try to persuade him to delay his departure a week or two. Tell him how important it is to your parents to see you married in your home town."

"I know how much you would like us to stay here longer, but I can assure you James is a determined man in carrying out his plans. I have agreed to his plan and I do not want to upset him by asking for changes."

"Very well," her father stated reluctantly, "you are set on doing as the two of you have planned. I for one will not try to persuade you further to make changes in your plan."

Karen too became conciliatory. "How long will you remain in Amsterdam and where will you go after you leave that city?"

Anna became calmer now that she had won her battle. "We will remain in Amsterdam only a week and then we will go to Scotland. James has a large estate near Edinburgh where we will live."

"I hope you will be able to come and visit us from time to time," Karen pleaded.

"Of course, I will. You know how much I will want to see both of you and my friends."

The emotional exchange between Anna and her parents over wedding plans had been preceded by a visit to Denmark of several weeks by the youthful James Hepburn, the 4th Earl of Bothwell and Lord Admiral of Scotland. Early in June 1560, Anna went to a pier in the Copenhagen port with her father and King Frederick to greet the visitor on his arrival.

Expectantly, Anna squinted through the morning sunlight, brilliantly reflected on the choppy sea, seeking to catch the first glimpse of the Scottish naval galleon coming southward toward Copenhagen down the narrow sea channel, the Oresund, separating Denmark from Sweden.

"I think I see the sail of the approaching Scottish ship," she exclaimed to her father who stood beside her talking seriously with King Frederick II about their expectations for meetings with the Lord High Admiral James Hepburn, 4th Earl of Bothwell from Scotland.

Her father turned toward his daughter and said, "Anna, you know many ships of various countries transit the Oresund. You have to see a ship at shorter range to identify the national flag it flies."

She continued scanning the sea, following the slowly enlarging form of the ship she had observed as it moved toward the port. She also tracked other ships that moved toward Copenhagen, seeking to identify the one of special interest. She saw a Swedish flag on the stern of the ship she first thought to be Scottish.

"You were right, father," she said to him. "I was mistaken about the identity of the ship I thought was the one we are expecting." She continued to study the many ships coming southward through the Oresund searching for the Scottish naval ship.

The seventeen-year-old Anna Trondson, youngest of the admiral's seven daughters, was eager to participate in welcoming the Scot to Copenhagen. Anna was an attractive brunette with light brown eyes, unlike the typical blond complexion of many others in her native Norway. Her long hair was dark brown and drifted casually around her shoulders. As she turned her head quickly from side to side, her long, unfettered hair swept wildly about her head and shoulders. She had a slender, appealing figure and dressed attractively. Her blue dress fit perfectly, the color matching her eyes and the sea. Her manner was open, pleasant and cheerful. Frequently, she was quite introspective but was given to bursts of speech when excited. In Copenhagen's social circles she had plenty of male friends but no one to whom she had become closely attached.

Anna thought it would be interesting to meet the distinguished young admiral. She had asked her father's permission to accompany him and the king in welcoming the visitor. Both the king and her father had agreed. For some time, she had been helping her father with routine functions of his office, and he had mentioned to her a few days earlier that the visiting nobleman was expected today, noting casually that, according to information gathered by the Danish navy, the Scottish admiral was unmarried, quite ambitious and much younger than might be supposed from his important assignment and distinguished titles.

Her young mind was active as she waited. Was the earl still unmarried, she wondered? Would she find him attractive and interesting? Perhaps he could fill a void in her mundane social life, a life currently lacking a man she really loved to be with. She would find answers to her questions at the earliest opportunity, maybe even today.

Although Anna watched the horizon intently, only occasionally did King Frederick or Admiral Kristoffer Trondson glance at the horizon for sight of the expected visitor's ship. They were too deeply involved in a conversation concerning naval matters to look often for the ship. Both of them knew that the English navy had recently imposed a blockade of the Firth of Forth, the important channel access to the port of Leith, near Edinburgh, Scotland. They also knew that English ground forces were simultaneously attacking Scottish military units along the southern border of Scotland. Although the Scottish Regent Mary was receiving some aid from France to help drive away the English blockade, she now sought assistance from the Danish navy in that struggle.

"The main question is," Frederick said to his naval aide, "what might the Scots offer us in exchange for any naval assistance we might provide them." He was eager to strengthen his own navy so that he might some day dominate the Baltic Sea where the Swedes now had the most powerful naval force in the region.

Trondson replied, "If the Scots could contribute something substantial to the strengthening of the Danish fleet, that would be of great interest to Denmark, but I cannot conceive what that might be."

"Perhaps they would agree to join with us in an alliance to help fight against the Swedes sometime in the future," the king suggested. "We will soon see what the envoy of the Scottish regent may be able to offer."

The king received a message yesterday indicating that the envoy, the Earl of Bothwell, had arrived in the Danish port of Elsinore, located north of Copenhagen. He was staying there a few days to obtain urgent repairs to his ship which was damaged in a storm while crossing the North Sea. Bothwell said he was leaving Elsinore this morning at 5 o'clock. Elsinore was only a few hours sailing time from Copenhagen.

"I find it significant," the king said, "that Bothwell was able to run successfully through the English blockade in the Firth of Forth."

Trondson replied, "I agree. He must be a skilled seaman and tactician to be able to escape that tight blockade."

Trondson glanced again at the horizon and said, "If this wind from the north continues, sir, I estimate that we shall see the Scot's ship within half an hour."

"I hope you are right, Admiral, because I have other important things to do today. and can't afford to wait very long for our visitor." The king was clearly impatient even though he had been on the pier less than half an hour.

Trondson sought to engage the king further in conversation so that he would not depart before the guest arrived. He said, "This Bothwell is quite a young man to carry the responsibilities entrusted to him by the Scottish Regent." As soon as he had spoken he regretted his remark, realizing that Frederick, himself, was only 25 years old, about the same age as the Scotsman.

Frederick ignored the remark, but commented that, "If he can offer us something significant, either in the short term or long term, our discussions could be worthwhile. Maybe, after Scotland's present struggle with the English, their navy could help us clear the waters around Denmark of pirates. In any case, Bothwell is obviously a very influential figure in the Scottish Government and it is important that we treat him with due respect."

Admiral Trondson was very pleased that the king had asked him to join in greeting the Lord High Admiral of Scotland. More importantly, he would also participate in the discussions with the visitor in the days to follow.

Trondson felt that his background would be extremely valuable in the discussions with the influential Bothwell. When the conversation with the king lagged, Trondson ruminated on his wide-ranging career. He took to the sea at an early age. In 1527, he was given command of a ship owned by his uncle, Archbishop Olav Engelbriktsson of Trondheim, Norway. In this role, one of Trondson's main tasks was to clear the seas around Norway of pirates. He learned a good deal about the activities of pirates and even found it to his advantage to become one himself for a time. In 1528-1529, the Danish king hired Trondson to pursue pirates in the seas around Denmark.

Some years later, Trondson was engaged by the Kaiser of Germany to help strengthen the German navy. The Kaiser made him a Marshall in the German forces. In 1542, however, Trondson again changed his affiliation and fought for the Danish king against Germany. In 1545, King Christian III made him an admiral in the Danish/Norwegian navy. Since 1387, Norway and Denmark had been joined in a union dominated by Denmark. The Danish king sent the Admiral and a fleet of ships to Iceland in 1551 to settle a local uprising. In the late 1550s, Trondson retired from the navy, and he now served King Frederick II as an advisor on a broad range of naval issues. Trondson knew his extensive naval experience would make him invaluable to the king during the talks with Bothwell.

As Bothwell stood on the top deck of his ship, slowly making its way toward Copenhagen, he too was reflecting on events that led to his important assignment from Regent Mary and what might be accomplished on her behalf. He was very eager to please her with a valuable agreement on naval cooperation between Denmark and Scotland. Scotland had an urgent need for naval assistance to deal effectively with the English blockade, and the Danish navy appeared to have the capacity to help. The key question: Was it in the strategic interest of King Frederick to help Scotland now?

The Scot was keenly aware of the English threat to the independence of Scotland. "If," he thought, "I could be instrumental through the forthcoming talks in saving Scotland from England's control of my country, I would earn a place in history for myself." He considered himself most fortunate to have the opportunity to achieve this historic goal.

Bothwell continued his speculations as his ship moved steadily toward the port of destination. If he succeeded in his efforts to save Scotland from English control, what sovereign would he serve, he wondered? Regent Mary of Guise was serving as acting head of the Scottish Government only temporarily; before long, the regent's daughter would take her place as Queen. He recalled the background: In 1542, King James V died just days after his wife gave birth to a daughter, Mary. The king's widow, called Mary of Guise, became Regent of Scotland upon his death. When her daughter was less than a year old, she was crowned Queen of Scotland. A few years later, the young Mary was sent to France for education and upbringing. When she was about 16 years of age, Mary was wed to Francis, the young son of King Henry II of France. When Henry died in 1559, Francis became king and Mary, of course, became Queen of France. At the same time, she was still

Queen of Scotland by inheritance. She did not, however, actually rule Scotland while serving as Queen of France.

In the spring of 1560, Mary of Guise, the Scottish Regent, was pressured by the English government to join England, effectively demanding that Scotland give up its independence. To help fend off these pressures, she received some minor assistance from France but nevertheless found it difficult to contend with the strong English forces facing Scotland, particularly the English naval blockade in the Firth of Forth. Seeking other assistance besides that of the French, the Regent agreed with King Frederick that the Lord High Admiral James Hepburn, the Earl of Bothwell, should visit the Danish king for the purpose of discussing possible naval cooperation that might be beneficial to both countries, particularly to Scotland in its struggle with the English. The Scottish admiral would arrive in Copenhagen about June 15, 1560, and would be prepared to enter into detailed discussions.

At the port of Copenhagen, the Danish king waited impatiently for the visitor's ship to arrive. He reflected on the problems he faced and wondered about the details of the Scottish admiral's proposals for naval cooperation. As the youthful head of state, the king was eager to surpass his late father's considerable achievements in the development and use of naval power. In King Frederick's vision, he could see the Danish navy dominating the entire Baltic area and extending its reach of power well beyond the Baltic Sea. Would an agreement with Scotland help him achieve that purpose? He would find out. Both the king and Trondson knew very well the importance of their continuing to make a careful assessment of the naval forces of all countries in the region. Frederick thought at least he could learn something of the strengths and weaknesses of the Scottish navy from the visitor. Admiral Trondson, who had served King Frederick's father well in building the Danish-Norwegian navy, now provided the new king advice on strategic planning for his naval forces. Thus he would be a full participant in the planned discussions.

As they waited on the pier, Anna did not interrupt the serious conversation between her father and the king. Instead, she mostly surveyed the sea to the north for sight of the expected ship. From time to time, for relief from the intense sunlight on the sea, she watched the growing bustle of port activity. She only projected herself into conversations of her father and the king when there was a lag in their exchanges.

"I think I now definitely see the Scottish ship," Anna suddenly exclaimed as her father was about to make another point in his discussion with Frederick. All eyes were then focused on the arriving ship, still at some distance.

"I believe you are right this time," the admiral said, "it carries a Scottish flag and is approaching from the right direction."

They watched the advancing ship in silence as it gradually appeared larger and more defined. Trondson recognized the characteristics of a Scottish-built galleon.

The brisk, steady wind held the sails full and firm as the ship quietly moved toward the harbor. On the main deck of the ship's bow stood a young man in a brilliant blue and silver officer's uniform. It was no doubt the Lord Admiral himself. The young officer ordered his crew to trim the ship's sails as they approached the pier. The ship then glided smoothly to a berth beside the welcoming party.

Once the lines secured the ship to the pier, the ship's crew quickly put a gang plank in place as the small welcoming group moved toward it. The Scottish visitor walked smartly down the gang plank and stepped onto the pier. He saluted King Frederick and Admiral Trondson. Then he bowed deeply to Anna. His manner was respectful and serious.

"Welcome to Denmark, Admiral," said the king. "I trust you had a pleasant voyage from Scotland?"

"Thank you, Your Highness. I cannot say the trip across the North Sea was exactly pleasant. Those waters are almost always rough and we had some damage to our rigging, which I had repaired in Elsinore. In contrast to sailing the rough conditions of the North Sea, coasting down the Oresund this morning was very enjoyable indeed."

"We are pleased to know that you successfully avoided attack from the English blockade around your country," the king added.

"That was indeed more of a challenge than the turbulent North Sea," Bothwell replied.

"Let me introduce the members of our welcoming group," the king said, turning first to his naval officer, "Admiral Kristoffer Trondson, my principal adviser on naval affairs."

"Very pleased to meet you sir," said the young officer, "I have heard impressive accounts of your naval engagements."

"It is a pleasure to meet an officer of the Scottish navy. I am sure we will have useful discussions about naval matters during your official visit in Denmark."

Anna had stood aside from the others, carefully watching every move of this good-looking officer. To her, he looked much like her father must have appeared in his youth, not tall or exactly handsome but nonetheless very attractive, strong and possessing a certain personal magnetism. Bothwell was of medium height and powerfully built. His brown eyes were intense and searching. She noticed that, while he concentrated his attention on the king and her father, he had cast glances at her a number of times with obvious interest.

"May I introduce Miss Anna Trondson," the king said. "She is a daughter of Admiral Trondson."

She smiled shyly and extended her hand. He looked at her intently, lifted her hand and kissed it politely, then continued to hold it for a few moments. Anna felt a glow and wished he could hold it longer.

"It is indeed a pleasure to meet the lovely daughter of Admiral Trondson," he said, seeming to compliment both Anna and her father.

"I am pleased to meet you," she said softly, looking directly into his eyes.

With the initial welcoming formalities completed, the king beckoned his guest to a waiting carriage. The gallant nobleman stepped aside and guided Anna into the carriage; then he slipped in beside her while the king and Trondson walked forward and boarded the king's own special carriage.

Quickly the two vehicles and various attendants and soldiers on horses sped toward the palace where the visitor was to stay during his visit. On the short ride to the palace, the young man spoke to Anna about his desire to see more of her in the coming days.

"King Frederick plans a party this evening in your honor and you shall have the opportunity to meet many of the court and other local people," she said, trying to shift attention away from herself, although she was definitely interested in seeing him again. In fact, it was difficult not to show her interest.

"I shall look forward to this social affair if I can be assured that you will be attending the event," he replied aggressively.

"I have been invited," she countered with studied ambiguity. The carriage had pulled up to the palace and an attendant was opening the coach door. She stepped out and he followed her. Momentarily, they stood beside the carriage looking at each other without speaking.

"Until tonight then!" said the Scottish admiral with complete confidence that she would be present that evening. He grasped her hand and kissed it, smiling faintly as he turned to follow an attendant inside the palace. She stood still for a moment, not sure whether to hurry away or watch his departure. Then, abruptly, she walked over to her father. Without saying a word about the visitor in the carriage, they were immediately transported to the Trondson mansion.

As she went to her room, Anna dreamily recalled what her father had told her about James Hepburn, 4th Earl of Bothwell and Lord Admiral of the Scottish Navy. He was born in 1535 in northern Scotland, the son of Patrick Hepburn, the 3rd Earl of Bothwell and Agnes Sinclair. He obtained his early education in the Palace of his uncle, the Bishop Patrick of Moray located at Spynie in northern Scotland. Following the fashion of the time, he was sent to France as a young man and spent a few years there studying military history and other subjects in a university. He learned to read, speak and write fluent French. When his father died in 1556, James returned to Scotland.

He succeeded to his father's titles which included Lord High

Admiral of Scotland, the Earldom of Bothwell and the Sheriff of Berwick, Haddington, Edinburgh and Bailie in Lauderdale. James's estate was in the Borders area, south of Edinburgh toward the border with England, and his principal home on the estate was called Crichton Castle, but the estate included the Hailes Castle, as well.

Her father had added that, although he considered himself a Protestant, James strongly supported the Roman Catholic Regent, Mary of Guise, in her struggle against the Protestant nobles in Scotland who were eager to see a change to a Protestant royal head of state. Now Regent Mary turned to the Earl of Bothwell as her representative to discuss naval affairs with the Danish king. His appointment may have been aided by the fact that James's father had been quite close to the Regent; he had courted her at one time. More to the point, however, James had been very helpful to the regent in certain of her encounters with enemies, both English military forces and certain opposition leaders among the Scots.

The elaborate party held in the palace on the night of the Scot's arrival in Copenhagen began with a reception line at which King Frederick II, the queen, and the visiting Scottish admiral stood at the head while an attendant nearby announced the name of each arriving guest. The king introduced the Scottish Admiral to a number of his more important guests.

Among those arriving early were Admiral Trondson, his wife Karen and daughter Anna. The Trondson family approached the king and queen as well as the Scottish visitor in the receiving line. After the formal introductions had been completed, the Scottish visitor said to Trondson and his wife, "I am especially pleased to see your charming daughter again." He looked directly at Anna and smiled broadly. Anna and her parents hesitated and then moved along quickly to let others in line meet the Scottish visitor. Her heart beat a little faster at this open attention.

A splendid banquet followed the reception. In the elegant dining room, careful attention was paid to protocol in seating arrangements. The king and queen sat, of course, at the head of the table. Members of the royal family and key military officers were assigned places near the king. Ambassadors were placed nearby and were seated according to a traditional order based on relative importance of the country represented and length of service of the ambassador. Other guests were seated more distant from the head table.

Because of Admiral Trondson's senior military standing, he, Karen and Anna were seated near the king. Much to Anna's delight, James Hepburn sat directly across the table from her.

"We meet again," he smiled.

Before he could enter into further conversation with Anna, waiters began serving an elaborate dinner featuring roast venison. For those who preferred something else, the waiters provided servings of suckling pig. Huge platters of meat and potatoes were brought to the guests and portions placed on the plates of each guest. Meanwhile, other waiters served from a large selection of French wines.

When Anna could again carry on a conversation free from the distractions of waiters, she tried to speak across the table.

"I hope you had a good rest today after your long journey." She said.

"Daytime rest is a luxury of the lazy or a necessity of the weak. I have been out exploring the city of Copenhagen. I find it very attractive."

Anna did not immediately reply and, in that moment, watched as the Ambassador from England, sitting on Admiral Bothwell's right, directed a pointed question to him. "Do you think Queen Mary of France spoke carelessly in asserting recently that she was next in line after Queen Elizabeth in her right to the throne of England."

Bothwell did not hesitate to answer the ambassador's impertinent question on the highly charged issue. The Scotsman's response was equally sharp. "Not at all. She might have said, with even greater justification, that her claim to the throne of England had priority over that of Elizabeth herself."

After that retort, the Ambassador turned away from the Scot and sought to engage others in conversation.

The Earl of Bothwell and the English Ambassador were both well aware of certain controversial statements of Queen Mary of France. She had indeed asserted that she stood second in line after her cousin Queen Elizabeth in succession to the English throne. Both men knew that this was a very serious issue in England. The English people had strong adverse feelings about the possibility of Mary ever becoming their queen, mainly because she was a Roman Catholic. The English people, predominately Protestant, were determined that England should never again become Catholic. In contrast, some fervent supporters of Mary Queen of Scots took the very partisan position questioning the legitimacy of Elizabeth as Queen of England, considering Mary more entitled to the English throne than Elizabeth!

The rival claims to the English throne had been a burning issue for many years in England and Scotland. Queen Mary of Scotland herself refused to concede that she had no claim to the English throne. Queen Elizabeth was a daughter of King Henry VIII and Anne Boleyn. In the eyes of Roman Catholics, Elizabeth was illegitimate because at the time of her birth, Henry VIII was still married to his previous wife, Catherine. Henry sought Catholic Church approval of his divorce from Catherine because she failed to produce a male heir. The Church refused the request. Henry then defied papal authorities and married Anne Boleyn. As to Mary's claim to the English throne, her grandmother, Margaret Tudor, was a sister of Henry VIII; thus Mary was in a key position for succession to the throne of England.

The issue of Mary's claim to the English throne, and particularly Queen Elizabeth's fear that Mary might somehow make good her claim, were to have profound effects on Mary Queen of Scots throughout her life. Might contention over this issue affect the lives of the Earl of Bothwell and Anna?

Relieved that his conversation with the person on his right was abruptly cut off, the Scottish admiral was about to speak again to Anna. Before he could do so, however, the Swedish Ambassador on his left spoke to him.

"What is the current strength of your Scottish navy, admiral?" He asked bluntly.

"Let me put it this way," the admiral said somewhat impatiently, "the strength of our navy is greater than that of Switzerland but less than that of Denmark."

"That is a wide range," the ambassador replied. "I presume the size of your fleet is near that of Denmark."

"That is correct but I do not intend to tell you how near."

That effectively ended the discussion about Scottish naval strength with the Swedish ambassador. James clearly had difficulty finding an opportunity to talk with Anna. Now that he had effectively closed the conversations with his two nearest neighbors, she was deeply involved in a discussion with others on her side of the table. Both Anna and he were frustrated.

When the banquet ended, the guests began moving about the dining hall. Attendants announced that there was to be dancing in the grand ballroom and many of the guests gradually drifted into the huge, beautifully decorated ballroom. Bothwell walked around the dining room and then entered the grand ballroom searching for Anna but could not find her.

Meanwhile, various people stopped to talk with him. Some were merely interested in polite conversation while others had specific questions to ask about Scotland's navy, the Scottish Royal family or major issues in international politics. James gave them all somewhat less than undivided attention as he continued to cast his eye about the rooms in search of the elusive woman who dominated his thoughts.

Finally, he spotted her in the ballroom dancing with an officer in the uniform of the Danish navy. An orchestra played a minuet and she danced beautifully, with obvious sensitivity to the music. Observing her graceful dancing made Bothwell all the more eager to be with her.

He placed himself strategically so that when the music stopped he could intercept the couple and claim her. The piece seemed interminable as he waited impatiently. When the musical selection ended, he hurried to her and requested a dance. Her partner excused himself and left, leaving Anna and the admiral studying each other for a moment.

"I thought you might have left the party. I searched for you everywhere."

"It is a large gathering so I am not surprised that you had difficulty finding me. But I am glad you did." she said.

The music began again and they danced in perfect harmony. They spoke little, satisfied for now to enjoy the pleasure of movement and music. He held her as close as he dared given the generally recognized decorum of the time and place.

After a time, he suggested they find a quiet spot where they could talk. Finding a secluded bench in the garden, they sat together and said nothing for some moments. It was a beautiful, warm summer night with the moon providing a soft light among the shadows.

"You look especially pretty tonight," he began, "I enjoyed the dance immensely. Now it is nice to just sit and talk awhile."

"You didn't seem particularly interested in talking with me at dinner and I assumed you had more weighty subjects on your mind than anything you might talk about with me," she said with a hint of irritation.

"Oh you are quite mistaken! I wanted desperately to talk with you but others around me insisted on carrying on conversations about their special interests. When I finally was free of them you were engaged in lively discussions with others. It was all very frustrating for me."

He could see that his plea for understanding was having a good effect. She began to smile and he felt all was forgiven.

"I too enjoyed the dance if not the dinner," she said with obvious sincerity. Then, looking toward the main exit she added, "I see the guests are beginning to leave and I know my father will be looking for me soon as he always likes to leave these affairs early."

"May I call you Anna?" he asked.

"Yes, all my friends do so," she replied.

"I would be pleased if you would call me James."

"Very well, James," she answered.

"Tell me about yourself. Where have you lived? What school did you attend? Do you like books, music and art?" Bothwell wanted to know all about her.

"You already know," she replied, "that my father is from Norway and you might surmise that I too originated there. That would be true. I was born in Trondheim, rather than on my parents' estate in the Hardanger Fjord. In fact, my family name of Trond originates in the area."

"Why was your family living in Trondheim?" he asked.

"Because my father was employed in Trondheim by Archbishop Englebriktson, to protect him during the period when tensions were very high between the Catholic Archbishop and the Protestant king over the reformation of the church of Norway."

"Why did you leave Trondheim?"

"A crisis developed in 1537 when I was still a baby. Threatened by a strong military force, my father transported the Archbishop and his entourage to Holland. My mother, grandparents, brothers and sisters and I also left. We then settled in Holland for two years."

"Where did you go after leaving Holland?" James asked.

"We lived in Bremen, Germany, for a few years while my father served the German Government as a naval officer. A few years later, we moved to Copenhagen. Wanting to hear about him, Anna concluded, "So you there have my life story in a nutshell." She reflected on his keen interest in her life story and thought he could be just the man she had been waiting for in her life.

"Well, I want to know more," he said. "What subjects do you like to study?"

"I am especially fond of geography. Having lived in Norway, Holland, Germany and Denmark, I wanted to know more about these and other places. Travel appeals to me very much."

"And have you studied modern languages?"

"Yes. In addition to the required Latin, I studied French and English."

"Then you are well prepared to travel many places. I can see you are restless to travel." Here, he thought, is a woman as fascinated as I am by the desire to travel.

"Now you know a lot about me. Tell me about yourself," she countered.

."Well, that will have to wait for another time," he replied. "I see your parents are ready to leave, but must you depart with them?"

"Yes, I must go," Anna said with frustration. She wanted to be with him longer.

Equally frustrated, he asked, "When can I see you again? Perhaps tomorrow evening? During the day I shall be occupied with a tour of naval facilities. But in the evening I shall come to your home and we can take a carriage ride along the waterfront."

"That would be nice. You may come at eight o'clock," she replied with relief as she hurried off to her father's waiting carriage.

During the next two weeks, Anna and James had many good times together. They took pleasant rides in the country, walked along the seashore, attended spirited parties, sat quietly in secluded places in the woods. On occasion, they went boating or horseback riding. There seemed to be no end to enjoyable activities to share. When they were not together, he was constantly on her mind. Meanwhile, during the day, he was intensely occupied with discussions of naval matters.

Anna learned a lot about James during their many evenings together and felt a growing attraction for him. He told her about his boyhood in Scotland, horseback riding, hunting, sailing and fishing. He told of the tutoring he received from relatives and others. As a teenager, he said, he was sent to France where he attended university, studying military science, the arts, various languages and other subjects. He told of his extensive travels to many places in Europe.

Anna could not help but exclaim, "I am impressed with the broad scope of your education and your extensive travel!" She was particularly captivated by the tales of his travels to various exotic cities. She herself longed to visit more such places. Perhaps some day she would do so.

One evening, while riding in a coach, he leaned over and kissed her. He presented her with a beautiful necklace. "Oh, how lovely!" she exclaimed. I shall treasure this necklace the rest of my life."

"It is a token of my love for you," he whispered and kissed her again, more passionately this time.

Over the next days as they traveled about the city and countryside, cozy in the secluded comfort of the comfortable leather seat, he held her tightly and expressed his love for her. "I shall love you always, Anna."

She looked into his eyes and responded tenderly, "What good fortune has come to me! Nothing could compare with the joy of falling in love with you, my dear James."

He held her even more tightly. "I have fallen completely in love with you. I hope we will be together forever."

"I could not live without you," she replied feeling a deep affection and completely in his control.

One day, James was free of the naval discussions and borrowed a small sail boat from a naval officer. Early in the morning, he appeared at the Trondson home and suggested to Anna that they go sailing in the Oresund, the strait between Copenhagen and the Malmo area to the east. It was a gorgeous summer day with bright sunlight and a strong, warm breeze.

"Oh, I would love to go sailing," she replied enthusiastically. "It seems a perfect day for it."

"I think it would be a fine day not only to sail but also to visit Malmo."

"Wonderful," she said. "I know some interesting places to visit over there."

A maid packed a lunch for the two of them and soon they were ready to ride to the harbor to board the ship. They cast off and the strong wind quickly took them far out into the Oresund.

"I love the sea," she told him, "especially when the weather is so perfect for sailing."

"Yes, and having you with me on such a day as this makes me particularly happy." He wrapped his arm around her and kissed her tenderly.

"I have never been so happy, my love," she replied looking into his eyes.

Soon, they arrived at the port of Malmo and tied the boat to a dock.

"Let's first go and visit the Malmohus, the recently rebuilt castle and fortress," Anna said. "I am sure we will be permitted to visit this important castle as the general in charge of it is a friend of my father."

"An excellent idea," James agreed. "Here, I see a carriage for hire. He can take us there." They rode through the bustling town toward the castle. On the way, they ate some of the lunch Anna's maid had prepared for them.

While en route, Anna exclaimed, "How wonderful it is to view our splendid Copenhagen from this vantage point." She looked wistfully toward the west across the Oresund.

"It is an impressive sight," James conceded.

Arriving at the castle, James asked the driver of the carriage to wait while they inquired about a visit.

James addressed a guard at the entrance, "Please inquire of General Johnson whether it would be convenient for Miss Anna Trondson and myself, Admiral Hepburn, to have a few words with him."

The guard disappeared and soon returned with General Johnson. "Good morning to both of you, Admiral Hepburn and Miss Trondson," the general greeted them warmly. "I know your father well, Miss Trondson."

"Let me introduce, Admiral Hepburn of Scotland," she replied. "He is on an official visit to King Frederick."

"I have heard of your visit and am very pleased to meet you, sir," General Johnson responded. "Would the two of you like to tour our castle? You are most welcome to do so. I shall be happy to show you around. Please follow me."

"You are most kind," Anna replied. They followed the general into the castle and he explained the design of the building, the furnishings and art work on display. The castle was built by King Eric in 1434 to strengthen Danish sovereignty over the Oresund and control Baltic trade. In 1542, King Christian III completed a major rebuilding of the castle employing the master Flemish builder, Morton Bussart.

"I am very impressed by its great size and beauty, "James said.

"And now would you like to have a cup of tea?" the general asked.

They accepted the offer and enjoyed an hour of interesting conversation about Malmo's history while drinking their tea. Then the visitors departed.

"That was a very worthwhile visit," James observed as they drove away from the castle in their carriage. "Some day, I hope to have a splendid a castle like that."

"Another place of interest is Lund where we can see a magnificent Romanesque cathedral," Anna said."

"Is it far from here?"

"No, this carriage can take us there in about an hour or two."

"All right. Let's go," he said.

On the way to Lund, they were able to see much beautiful scenery. The weather continued warm and sunny. Arriving in Lund they first stopped at an inn to relax and have some refreshments.

When they went to see the cathedral a bishop explained to them the history of the town and the fine cathedral building. King Canute had founded the town in 1020. In the 12th century, the main part of the cathedral was built. It was later enlarged and improved. An impressive spire soared high into the sky.

"As you can see," the bishop related, "these beautiful stained glass windows tell familiar biblical stories or feature prominent biblical personalities including disciples."

"Thank you so much for your fine tour," Anna said to the bishop as they stood at the exit. "It is getting late and we must now return to Malmo."

Anna and James snuggled together in the back of the carriage during the long ride in the cool, late afternoon while returning to the Malmo port.

"Our day in Malmo and Lund has been an unforgettable time for me," Anna said. "Thank you, darling, for showing me such a good time."

"It was you who directed me to the Malmo castle and the Lund Cathedral. I enjoyed both of these places. Actually, wherever we go, I enjoy being with you." He kissed her.

It was dusk when the two lovers sailed from Malmo toward Copenhagen. The wind was not so favorable for their return as it had been during the morning crossing, but James was quite skilled in sailing and made the most of the limited wind available. It was dark when they arrived at the Copenhagen harbor, dimly lit by a beacon to guide ships to the port.

"Here we are, sweetheart," James said as they found their berth. "Come, I will help you out of the boat."

They found a carriage and soon arrived at Anna's home. While the carriage waited, James took her to the door.

"Thank you again for a wonderful day, darling," Anna said. "I could not have been happier."

"It really was wonderful to have a full day with you, my sweet." He hugged her and gave her a long kiss before she departed into the house.

Most days in Copenhagen, James was occupied with lengthy discussions of naval matters. Early in July, however, these discussion were temporarily suspended as Bothwell stated to the Danes that Regent Mary had asked him not only to visit Denmark but also Germany and attempt to recruit some German mercenaries for Scotland. The king and Trondson accompanied Admiral Bothwell to Germany for these special talks which were soon thrown off track.

A few days after their arrival in Germany, the German Kaiser told his visitors, "I have important but sad news for you. We have just been informed by a ship captain from Scotland that the Regent, Mary of Guise, died on June 11, 1560, in Edinburgh. I want to express my sadness in having to convey the news of this tragic loss. Admiral Bothwell, please convey to your leaders in Edinburgh our expressions of Germany's sorrow over the country's great loss."

The stunned Bothwell replied, "Thank you sir, I am shocked to hear this unfortunate news. She has been my strong, and dependable supporter in Scotland. I shall miss her greatly."

He wondered what this meant for Scotland's future leadership and his own future. Would the regent's daughter, Mary, now take an active role as Scottish Queen as was her right, moving to

Edinburgh from Paris? What would the French people think of the queen of France relocating to Edinburgh? Since this seemed unlikely, would Lord James Stuart of Moray now become the new regent?

"I should add," the Kaiser continued, "that the allies, Scotland and France, have concluded a treaty of peace with England. As a result of this treaty, England is withdrawing its blockade of the Firth of Forth and withdrawing soldiers from the borders area of Scotland. I see no need for Scotland to employ mercenaries from Germany."

King Frederick then observed, "In view of this treaty, Admiral, the Scottish government will have no need for naval support from us."

"You are probably right, sir," Bothwell acknowledged. "I shall have to consult my government for further instructions in view of these changed circumstances. In the meantime, I too see no reason for further official talks."

The news of the regent's death, and the treaty that quickly followed, effectively ended Bothwell's mission to Denmark. On his return to Copenhagen from Germany, he made preparations to leave the country.

One warm pleasant evening, Anna and James were walking again in the palace garden as they did the first night they were together. She was disconsolate, reflecting on the wonderful times the two of them had enjoyed and saddened to think now about his impending departure. He, too, expressed his disappointment that events had forced an approaching end of a perfect visit, especially his delightful evenings and Sundays with her.

Suddenly, James stopped and exclaimed, "I have a wonderful idea! You and I will go to Amsterdam together. We will have great fun in that fantastic city. I have been there a number of times and I can promise you that no city of Europe compares with Amsterdam. We will get married there and have our honeymoon in the same exciting town. When we are ready to leave, we will go to Scotland and live on my estate. What do you think? Are you willing?"

Anna at first was speechless! She was breathless, dizzy with excitement. "I am overwhelmed!" She did not have to think before adding, "What a marvelous idea! Yes! Yes! Of course I will go with you!" They embraced and he held her a long time. She knew she loved him so much that she would go anywhere in the world with him.

He kissed her passionately! The long kiss and tight embrace seemed to seal the lover's agreement that they would spend their lives together, first in the appealing Amsterdam and then in Scotland. She could not imagine anything more attractive and satisfying.

Anna had to explain their plan to her parents. She knew that would be difficult. Carefully, she managed to find a time when both her parents were relaxed and seemed to be in a positive frame of mind.

"As you know," she began hesitantly, "since the talks between James and Danish officials have ended, James will be leaving soon. I am sure you realize now that he and I are very much in love. Furthermore, he has asked me to marry him and I have agreed."

"Why that is wonderful!" Anna's mother cried. "I have indeed seen a dramatic change in you since he came to town."

When Anna further explained that they were going to elope to Amsterdam rather than marry in Copenhagen the Trondson parents were not at all pleased, but it soon became apparent to them that the young couple was determined to carry out their plan. Therefore her parents wished them happiness in their new life together.

Two days later, Anna boarded the Scottish warship and stowed her things in a cabin. With mixed feelings, her parents on the pier bid the young couple a tearful goodbye as they set sail and departed Copenhagen.

CHAPTER 2

Enjoyable Times in Amsterdam

"Tell me again what route we take to Amsterdam," Anna asked James as they departed Copenhagen port. "Will we stay close to the shore or venture further out to sea?" She was thrilled that they were on their way to the Dutch city aboard the "Edinburgh."

"We'll first go northward through the restricted waters of the Oresund, then northwestward through the Kattegut and later westward through the Skagerrak to the rougher waters of the North Sea. We need to stay well off shore to avoid the hazards of striking rocks in shallow water."

"Then, I suppose," she added, "we will sail southward past Jutland and the Friisian Islands and shortly enter the Amstel River."

"You are right. Amsterdam is only a short distance up the Amstel River."

Despite her anticipation of good times ahead, Anna was sad leaving home and parents. The touching image of her parents on the dock waving goodbye lingered in her mind. James noticed that she harbored a little sadness and held her tightly, reassuring her that they were at the beginning of a great adventure together.

"How great it is to be out on the sea again!" he exclaimed. "Doesn't that brisk wind feel refreshing?" Although the air was cool, the morning sunlight was brilliant.

"Yes. I, do, enjoy the sea," she said. "My father often took me with him on board his ships." She was still a bit melancholy when she thought of her parents at home. But her joy of being here with James far outweighed any sadness.

"Come, let us go below and have breakfast," James suggested.

"It should be ready now." He took her arm and led her to a lower deck.

Nightfall arrived as they entered the North Sea and then shifted direction southward. Fortunately, the sea was not as rough as is often experienced by ships sailing these waters.

Late in the evening, James and Anna were served dinner of chicken and dumplings. A bottle of French wine was taken from the ample supply in the wine chest. Both of them drank a great deal of wine in celebration of their voyage and became quite merry. They felt they had much to celebrate!

"Oh my," Anna said softly but happily, "I believe I am drunk." She smiled mischievously.

"I'm glad you are enjoying the wine, my love. So am I." He was more accustomed to drinking wine than she and could better control himself when drinking in excess. Pulling her close to him, he circled his arm around her waist and kissed her. She melted in his arms.

He began to remove her dress but she resisted, saying, "No, please don't do that!" She and James had never been intimate in Copenhagen. "Not until we are married," she pleaded.

"What difference does it make?" he answered. "Only the two of us will know, and we both want to express our love for each other fully."

"But I would rather wait," she replied weakly. He knew she would soon give in to him. Slowly and gently he removed all her clothes and she did not stop him. Then he quickly undressed and carried her to a nearby bunk.

They lay side by side briefly as he fondled her. She responded reluctantly. She knew they should wait until they said their vows, but with a sense of guilt, she also felt her body longing for his touch. As James became increasingly excited, he moved above her. Shortly, he felt a satisfying climax. Anna, however, was more disturbed. It all happened so quickly, and her reluctance kept her from responding completely. James was soon asleep.

Now, as he slept, her thoughts were troubled. She could not help being angry that James had pressed her this far so soon. Why did he not respect her wish to wait? Was it part of his nature to override her wishes?

She remained awake, wondering whether she had been too easy a conquest, and whether he had been disrespectful of her wishes. It was some considerable time before she too could sleep.

Through the night, the ship sailed southward past Jutland and the Friisian Islands and then, in the early morning, the ship entered the Amstel River. Ships flying the flags of many countries passed them in both directions up and down the Amstel River, an indication of the large amount of international commerce handled in the important port of Amsterdam. The thriving city lay along the river only a few miles from the sea. Both Anna and James were on the deck of the "Edinburgh," admiring the variety of ships in the harbor and the boisterous activity on the docks.

"Is Amsterdam dangerous?" she asked nervously.

"No, it is comparatively safe," he replied reassuringly.

"Compared to what?"

"To the countryside. As you know, Spain is persecuting Protestants in the low countries, a severe reaction to the Reformation that is spreading rapidly in much of northern Europe. Spain controls a large part of the territory here and is determined to force the people to remain Catholic or become Catholic. Most of the trouble is in the countryside. Amsterdam is largely left alone. This city is very important commercially and the rulers do not want to ruin that trade."

"I am glad there is not trouble in the city," Anna said.

"In recent years," James noted, "Holland has become one of the most important trading countries in the world and it's commercial fleet is unrivaled. Amsterdam is not only the center of a vibrant international trade but is also noted for its impressive cultural activities. Many foreigners are attracted to the city not only for trade but also for these other reasons."

James stood on the deck, Anna beside him, taking in the sights of the city as they made their final approach to the port. The vitality of the port was exciting with stevedores, passengers, ship crews and others moving about with vigor and determination. The admiral found an open berth and eased his ship to the pier.

"What a busy place this is!" Anna exclaimed as they watched the stevedores, traders, ship crews, travelers and others moving about the port.

"It's even more active than the last time I was here," James noted. As a naval officer, the admiral was, of course, a well-traveled man. Reflecting on his visit here last year, he thought Amsterdam was the most stimulating of all European ports.

His skillful crew acted efficiently in bringing the ship into a berth and securing the ship to the moorings. The gang plank was lowered and all was ready for the admiral and his companion to disembark. In contrast to his arrival in Copenhagen, there was no welcoming party in Amsterdam. James and Anna were here on a strictly private, visit and that is the way they wanted it.

The Admiral addressed his first officer, "We shall be in the city for some hours. We will locate an inn and arrange for rooms. Then I will send for our trunks from the ship. You can expect someone to come for them sometime this afternoon."

"Aye Sir! And when will the admiral sail from Amsterdam?"

"I'll return later in the day and discuss our plans at that time."

James and Anna then walked a short distance to an area of the city where there was a cluster of inns. Not surprisingly, the inns were located near the port for the convenience of the many travelers who arrived in Amsterdam by ship and departed the city in the same way.

James recognized the inn where he had stayed during an earlier visit and they contacted the owner. The innkeeper had a large suite of rooms on the second floor with a fine view of the harbor. He showed the rooms to the couple. From a large window in the room, one could see a pretty garden beside the inn where many flowers bloomed.

"I think this is just the right place for us, Anna!" James said enthusiastically.

Anna hesitated for a moment, noting that there was only one bed in the two-room suite. Since they were not yet married, she disliked the impropriety of sharing the bed with her fiance. Then she considered the fact that they had already been intimate on the ship. She also rationalized that no one in Amsterdam, so far as she knew, was aware of her presence in the city and therefore she was not likely to be embarrassed. The final comforting thought rushing through her mind was that they would be married in only a day or two anyway and it would certainly be convenient to be settled in one place for the duration of their stay in Amsterdam.

The innkeeper stood tensely in the doorway eager for a favorable decision. It was not often that he could rent this comparatively expensive suite with its bedroom and sitting room.

"Yes, it is lovely!" she said to James. The innkeeper relaxed and a wide smile came over his face. James was obviously pleased with the quick decision on the rooms.

He swept her off her feet. "We are going to have the time of our lives in Amsterdam my love," he said, "You will see."

"Yes sweetheart, I know we will!" she replied. She was completely in love with him and wanted to do everything she could to make him happy.

Arrangements were made with the innkeeper to pick up the trunks at the ship. Then James and Anna went to the dining room and had a glass of wine to celebrate their arrival in Amsterdam. A long leisurely lunch of roast duck followed.

"Now I had better return to the ship and give instructions to my first officer concerning the ship," James announced. "In the meantime, the trunks should now be in the room and you can unpack them."

"Do you still plan to send the ship to Scotland?" she asked.

"Yes. I cannot hold this valuable ship here for long. It is expected soon in Scotland for other duty. When we are ready to leave Amsterdam, I will have little difficulty finding passage for us on a commercial ship that will take us to Scotland." He left the inn and Anna went to their room.

While she unpacked, she wondered vaguely why he could not have spent this extra time in Copenhagen rather than Amsterdam. They could then have wed before departing on their journey to Scotland. She was so in love, however, that she brushed the thought away. She knew he must have very good reasons

That evening, Anna and James went to dinner late and enjoyed an excellent meal of roast lamb and an expensive red wine from France. The food was especially appreciated after eating the limited fare available aboard ship. The atmosphere of the dining room was convivial, even boisterous. Musicians played local folk music which many of the patrons knew well and joined in singing. They danced with great spirit and Anna and James also joined in the dancing. It was very late when James suggested that it was time to leave. They went to their suite and soon made love. Having now accepted the situation, and knowing they would soon be husband and wife, Anna could relax and fully return his passion. They then slept soundly until morning.

The next day and for days thereafter, Anna and James found many ways to entertain themselves in this spirited city. They dined in various inns, danced at a festival, attended theater performances, took rides in carriages, rode on horseback into the countryside, walked along the seashore and strolled in beautiful gardens. They enjoyed these activities immensely and grew closer.

A week passed. As they were having lunch one day, Anna became pensive in a relaxed moment and said to James, "We have had wonderful times these past several days and I hesitate to suggest any changes. Still, I recall that our plan for Amsterdam included something else as well."

"You mean our getting married, right?"

"Yes, dear, I do. I look forward to it so much!"

"Of course, as do I. We must do so soon. Tomorrow I shall see to the arrangements."

"Wonderful, I am so happy."

In the early afternoon of the following day, James told Anna that he was going out to find a magistrate and make arrangements for the marriage. Late in the afternoon, he returned and told the disappointed Anna that he had not been successful in locating a magistrate but would try again the next day.

The following afternoon, he again went out in search of an official to perform the marriage. He returned to the inn late in the day.

"I finally found a magistrate who can marry us but he will be out of the city for a few days."

"But surely," Anna said expectantly, "there must be more than one magistrate available to perform a marriage in a city of this large size."

"You are probably right about that, and I shall keep trying. Perhaps I shall have better luck tomorrow."

Anna was disappointed at the unexpected delay in the wedding which she thought was so near when they arrived in Amsterdam. At the same time, she realized that they were in an unfamiliar city where one could not so easily arrange a marriage as in one's home country. Maybe her parents had been right. She and James loved each other more than ever, so she resolved to be patient. In the meantime, they continued their whirl of activity, leaving her little time to dwell on her disappointment over the delay in the marriage.

James apparently continued to pursue a magistrate who could perform the ceremony, but each time he returned with a negative report for one reason or another.

Nearly two weeks had passed since their arrival. One morning, James was quiet and looked very worried. Anna noticed this unusual mood.

"What is troubling you, my darling? You look very concerned about something."

"Anna, I am very disturbed about my funds, or rather the lack of them. I had considerable money when we arrived here but it all seems to have vanished."

"Oh, I had no idea you were having this difficulty. You should have told me sooner. I brought a little money with me and you can have some of it," Anna offered.

"The immediate problem is that the innkeeper is pressing me for payment of the rent and I do not have it."

She reached for her purse, found some silver coins and handed them to him.

"I feel terrible taking money from you. I shall return it very soon. In the meantime, I will use this money to pay for our suite. This money is a big help but it does not solve my financial problem.

I have thought through the situation very carefully and have decided the best solution is for me to go to Paris where I have friends who will advance me funds."

"Go to Paris?" she said anxiously. He was silent for a moment and then she asked, "May I go with you?"

"I shall be gone only a week, my dear," he consoled. It would be best if you wait here until I return. While I am gone, you can, if you like, follow-up with the magistrate I contacted and fix a time and place for the wedding."

She tearfully agreed to wait for him in Amsterdam.

"How soon will you leave?" she asked with sadness in her voice.

"My need for funds is so urgent I think it best if I leave as soon as I can arrange transportation. If I can find a carriage going to Paris today, I shall do so. The sooner I leave, the sooner I will return and we will be back together."

Anna began to cry but after a few minutes she composed herself. James went downstairs to the innkeeper, paid the bill and asked about the availability of a carriage to Paris. In a few minutes, he was able to make a reservation for departure early that afternoon.

James returned to Anna and together they packed some things for his journey. Then they talked a long time about their future life together. He described his estate in detail and what her responsibilities would be as his wife. He then expanded about the wonderful social life she could expect in Scotland. Shortly before the carriage was scheduled to depart, they walked together to the waiting carriage.

"I shall miss you Anna my sweet but we will be together again in a week."

"Goodbye, my darling. I shall miss you too and will look forward to your return as soon as possible." He kissed her and then he quickly entered the carriage.

As the carriage slowly pulled away, Anna waved goodbye and prayed for his early return.

The three day trip to Paris was hardly a pleasant one. It involved two overnight stops at inns that were distinctly inferior to the inn where he and Anna stayed in Amsterdam.

James was well aware that the area through which he would be traveling was torn by religious strife, that is, the raging conflict between the Protestant Reformation and Catholic Counterreformation. Many Protestants were severely persecuted in this region which was dominated by Catholics. As a Protestant, James was vulnerable. He was not hesitant about taking risks, however, and brushed off any danger that might lie ahead.

Two men were fellow passengers with Bothwell. They introduced themselves to Bothwell and, from time to time, the three of them engaged in conversation about Paris and other subjects of common interest. The discomfort of the arduous journey was somewhat relieved by these conversations. One passenger was a merchant from Paris and the other a student at the Sorbonne returning to Paris after a visit in Amsterdam. The conversation gave Bothwell an opportunity to practice French, a language he had learned well some years earlier when he was a student in Paris, but the limited opportunity to use the language in Scotland during the past four years resulted in some loss in his ability to speak it. With the practice gained on the journey, he soon felt confident speaking French again.

The rough road made the carriage ride extremely uncomfortable. By sundown the three passengers were clearly ready for a rest. The coach stopped at the Boar's Inn, a wretched, uninviting place located in the small community of Estende.

Bothwell was the first to appear at the desk to obtain a room assignment. The unkempt innkeeper gave him a key and directed him to the sparse room. Exhausted from the bumpy ride, James lay down on the bed and was soon asleep. A few hours later, he awoke, washed himself and then found the innkeeper's wife who gave him some soup, bread and a stein of beer. Feeling the need for exercise, he then went for a short walk along the road beside the inn. In the moonlit night, he was able to see just well enough that he did not stumble or lose his way. After awhile, he reversed his direction and returned to the inn, guided by the candle light in a window of the inn. Before long, he was asleep for the night.

Early the next morning as the sun was about to appear above

the horizon, the carriage was ready to continue the journey toward Paris. The three passengers entered the coach and took their seats. Soon the horses were urged to begin what would become another very long and tiring day. Fortunately, the weather was good and thus they were able to travel somewhat faster than would have been the case in heavy rain, which often occurred at this time of year.

At the end of the long day, as darkness descended on another small village, the carriage came to a stop at an inn along the road, their place to spend the night, The Louise Inn. Operated by a woman and her daughter, the inn was somewhat more appealing than the inn where they stayed the previous night, this one being well-built, small, clean and a bit rustic. More important, a good meal was served by the woman innkeeper and her daughter. Though very tired from the trip, Bothwell was clearly in a much better frame of mind here than at the previous place.

After a night of rest for travelers, driver and horses, the carriage pulled up in front of the inn at sunrise ready to continue the journey toward their final destination. Arriving at last in Paris, Bothwell was dropped off at a street corner that he readily recognized. He bade goodbye to his companions and proceeded to find a tavern where he could refresh himself after the rugged trip. He was tired and dusty and found a tavern in a nearby inn. Two steins of beer rejuvenated him. Sitting in the tavern, he worried that he might have more difficulty in raising funds from friends than he had suggested to Anna. While he did have friends in Paris, it had been a long time since he had seen them and they might be less willing to help him than he had implied.

CHAPTER 3

Anna Remains in Amsterdam

While James is in Paris

The admiral's most urgent need was to find an inexpensive room where he could stay while he undertook his search for funds among friends around town. He thought momentarily that he might conserve his limited cash reserves by asking a friend if he could stay with him as a courtesy. Uncertain, however, whether any of these friendships was close enough that they would honor such a request, he wondered whether he could afford to stay in an inn. In the end, he decided that it would be best not to test his old friendships by requesting them to provide a room but rather simply stay in a cheap inn. He soon found Robert's Inn, a modest place, not far from the spot where he had left the carriage.

After a good night's sleep, James felt refreshed and in better spirits than he did on arrival here. He planned his activities over the next few days. After careful consideration, he decided that his highest priority was to arrange a meeting with Queen Mary, not to seek a loan from a friend. He felt that his career might well be advanced in some way through a contact with her. Since the queen's late mother, Regent Mary of Guise, had been friendly toward him and had given him the important recent assignment to Denmark, he thought he could establish a useful relationship with Queen Mary.

James had never met the young queen and was eager to do so. This eighteen year old was known to the Scottish people as Mary Queen of Scots. For the past two years, however, she was also the wife and queen of the youthful King Francis II of France. She had lived in France for several years and had many relatives and friends here. Mary felt entirely comfortable in this situation.

Admiral James Hepburn knew that Mary's late mother, the regent, expected Mary to return to Scotland eventually and reside there. But now it appeared that she would continue to live in France indefinitely as Queen of France. A devout Catholic, she was among people here who were almost universally of that faith. Were she to live in Scotland where the people were largely Protestant, she would not find life so congenial. Because of her religion, she knew that she was not universally liked in the country of her birth.

The Earl of Bothwell felt that his knowledge of France and the French language along with his loyalty to Scotland would enable him to communicate well with Queen Mary. After all, he had been educated in France and spoke French reasonably well. At the same time, he was a Scotsman with a proven record of loyalty to the royal family of Scotland. He was confident he could establish a good relationship with her royal highness if given a chance.

Bothwell's need for money was, of course, urgent. And it was not just a case of being temporarily short of cash while on the continent as he had told Anna. His financial circumstances were more precarious than that. In Scotland, although he was a nobleman with important titles, he had mounting debts and only a modest income. He was well aware that although he owned a large estate in southern Scotland, there were significant claims against it tracing back to his father's spendthrift ways and unsuccessful financial transactions. Despite these poor financial circumstances, the young earl greatly enjoyed living well beyond his means, like his father. Thus he had an overwhelming desire to advance his career in terms of wealth and position. He recognized that wealth and political power usually go together and he was eager for both of them. A visit with Queen Mary as soon as possible fit perfectly into his plans.

He prepared a message to the queen.

"Her Majesty Mary Queen of Scots:

"As one of your loyal subjects and a humble servant in the service of your majesty's Navy, I respectfully request a meeting with you at your earliest convenience. On behalf of your late mother, Regent Mary of Guise, I recently completed an official visit to King Frederick in Copenhagen with the objective of exploring potential cooperation between the naval forces of Scotland and Denmark. Before returning to Scotland, I came to Paris for the purpose of visiting friends. A meeting with your majesty prior to my return to Scotland would be a great honor for me. I am in a position to report on the strength of Scottish naval forces as compared with the strength of other naval forces in northern Europe.

Signed, Lord Admiral James Hepburn, 4th Earl of Bothwell
Robert's Inn, Etoille Avenue, Paris
August 3, 1560"

He walked the considerable distance from his inn to the St. Germain-en-Laye Palace. Dressed in his impressive admiral's uniform, Bothwell presented himself to the chief of the palace guard. The guard saluted the visitor smartly. Then the admiral handed him the sealed envelope containing his message for the queen.

"See that this message is delivered to Queen Mary as soon as possible," he said with authority.

"Yes Sir. I will have it delivered immediately."

Bothwell hurried away, not waiting for a reply. If she replies as he expected, a message would be delivered to him at his inn in due course. Returning to the inn, he considered carefully what he would say during the anticipated meeting with the queen.

He realized that many people seek appointments with royal heads of state and therefore some delay in securing an appointment might well be expected. At least he was assured that the queen was present in the palace; otherwise the guard would not have stated that he would deliver the message promptly. Bothwell had been

somewhat apprehensive that she might not be in the palace since
the royal family often travels around the country to keep contact
with the people and listen to grievances. He was encouraged by
what the captain of the palace guard had inadvertently revealed to
him.

Mid-morning of the following day, a messenger from the palace
delivered an envelope to him at the Roberts Inn and he eagerly
ripped open the envelope. The message was addressed to The Lord
Admiral James Hepburn, 4th Earl of Bothwell, and read:

> "The queen will be pleased to see you in the near future
> when a suitable time can be arranged. We will advise you
> soon of the date and time."

> Signed, Andre Gilet, Secretary to Her Majesty,
> Mary Queen of Scots
> August 4, 1560"

Bothwell was pleased at the positive tone of the message but
disappointed that no definite time for the meeting had been fixed.
A week passed. He still could not bring himself to visit friends. He
was bored waiting and considered finding some woman for
company, but his funds were so limited he could not afford the
entertainment he desired.

Finally, he was advised in another message from the palace
that a meeting had been set for August 30th at three PM in the
Orleans Palace, almost a full month after his arrival in Paris. The
appointment was none too soon as his funds were nearly exhausted.
Having little else to do, he spent a great deal of time preparing for
the impending visit with the queen. During this wait, he gave
little thought to Anna or her possible need for funds in Amsterdam.
When she did come to mind, his view was, "What can I tell her? I
have no idea when I can return to Amsterdam and I certainly have
no money for her. I barely have enough money to live here."

He was convinced that the meeting with the queen was to be
such an important occasion, such a rare opportunity, it behooved

him to plan well for an effective presentation to the queen. His entire career depended on it. Although the queen would no doubt determine the subjects to be discussed, Bothwell thought he could adroitly steer the meeting to the subjects he had already suggested to her, that is, the naval forces of northern Europe including the Scottish Navy. His main source of information was his recollection of key information developed in the official meetings in Copenhagen on naval problems. Bothwell carefully reviewed his thoughts concerning the strengths and vulnerabilities of the naval forces in various states of northern Europe. Also, he reviewed his knowledge of the strengths and limitations of the naval forces of the Scottish Navy.

On the day of the meeting with the queen, he had his uniform and boots cleaned and his hair trimmed. He was tense. To relax before the meeting, he had a couple of glasses of wine in the tavern of Robert's Inn.

At the appointed time, Bothwell arrived at the palace gate and showed the guard his message. The guard had already been informed of his impending arrival.

"Come this way, sir." A guard ushered him into the drawing room. The queen's secretary appeared.

"Please wait here a few moments, sir," the secretary said. Bothwell was on edge.

To Bothwell's surprise, King Francis as well as Queen Mary entered the room and the admiral bowed deeply to the royal couple. How young they both were! He had known, of course, that the king was only sixteen and the queen eighteen, but nevertheless he was struck by their youthful appearance. She was taller than he expected, taller than himself, and very attractive. Her fine clothes and regal bearing made her very much a queen. Francis was physically much less impressive.

"Good afternoon Admiral," they greeted him in turn. Then she said in a soft voice, "I am delighted to see someone from Scotland."

"It is a great honor to meet you both," Bothwell responded evenly.

"King Francis wanted to meet you, but he will not be able to attend our meeting," the queen said.

"Had I the time," the king said, "I would like to participate in your discussions but other urgent matters demand my attention. In any case, the queen is better informed on the subjects you will discuss." The king then left the room and Bothwell bowed again as he departed.

Queen Mary sat down in a chair by her desk and motioned for Bothwell to take a seat nearby.

"What news do you have from Scotland?" she began. Then, before he could reply, she added, "I realize, of course, that you have been away from our homeland many weeks."

"The most disturbing news from Scotland, which I recently received while in Germany, was the unfortunate and untimely death of your mother. She was most generous in appointing me to represent her in discussions in Copenhagen with King Frederick. Permit me to extend my sincere sympathies to you on your loss."

"Thank you. All of us, and especially myself, feel the loss intensely," she said with obvious sadness. She hesitated a moment and then, after regaining her composure, continued. "The past two years have been a time of considerable political confusion in Scotland, particularly during the month or so following my mother's death. I have been informed that you were a loyal supporter of my mother in Scotland. Your mission to Denmark was clear evidence of your loyalty to her and the high regard she had for your capabilities."

"I was honored to support Her Highness in Edinburgh and to serve on that mission."

"You suggested in your message that the principal subject of our discussion might be the naval forces of Scotland and certain other countries. I know you can speak authoritatively on that subject and it is a matter of considerable interest to me." They talked for some time about naval forces and she was impressed with his extensive knowledge of the relative strength of various naval forces.

"Following your request for an appointment, we made certain inquiries about your service to Scotland, and we believe we may, in the near future, have further need for your service, service which I am not yet prepared to discuss. For the present, King Francis and I are agreed that you should be named a Gentleman of the King's Chamber and we shall inform you soon what service we will require of you."

Bothwell was surprised at this good news and expressed his profound appreciation. Then he said, "I shall be leaving for Amsterdam tomorrow and will sail from that city to Scotland as soon as possible. Therefore, I can soon be reached in Edinburgh."

"I'll contact you through officials in Edinburgh when I need you. Incidentally, I should add that a Gentleman of the King's Chamber carries a salary. I do not recall the amount but, in any case, I should like to give you now a present of six hundred crowns in recognition of your past service to my mother." She rose to leave and handed him a pouch of coins.

Bothwell rose too and replied, "I am indeed grateful for your confidence in me and for this generous present."

"I must leave you now but we will meet again soon." With a grand gesture she indicated that the meeting was at an end.

"Thank you your majesty, I will be ready to undertake whatever service you will require of me. It will be a great honor to do so." He bowed deeply.

As Bothwell left the palace, he could hardly contain his exuberance. Not only had he received an important appointment from the king and queen, but also he had obtained a promise of some further unspecified service that he would likely undertake.

And incredibly, he marveled, she presented him with a gift of six hundred crowns! He could not have been more fortunate in his first meeting with Queen Mary. He was convinced that he had made a good impression on the queen. In fact, it seemed to him that he had actually charmed Mary Queen of Scots. His magic with women had worked again, he told himself.

Bothwell returned to the Robert's Inn and made arrangements to leave Paris the following day. Now, there was clearly no need to see friends and borrow money from any of them.

Having money in hand, he was now prepared to return to

Amsterdam and see Anna again. He anticipated that she probably
would be quite upset when he finally returned after so long a delay.
He decided to give her a present as a means of placating any ill
feelings. Not far from his inn, he found a shop where he bought a
necklace. "I suppose," he contemplated, "she is lonesome and will
probably be eager to see me in any case. Perhaps I should have sent
her a letter explaining that my return was being delayed. But how
could I think of everything? And, anyway, I did not know until
yesterday when I could leave Paris." Only now, as he made
arrangements for his return, did he think about how long he had
been absent and wonder whether she had sufficient funds to cover
living expenses during the long period he had been in Paris.

CHAPTER 4

Anna and James Together Again in Amsterdam

When James departed Amsterdam for Paris early in August, Anna felt very sorry for him. She visualized him bumping along on rough roads in the uncomfortable carriage, stepping out of the coach at the end of each day exhausted, and sleeping in poor quality inns on overnight stops. She hoped he would be cheered by seeing his friends in Paris.

Returning to the inn, Anna felt very lonesome. She wondered how she could bear the wait of a whole week. She thought about the suggestion James made that she find a magistrate and arrange a marriage date. She wondered how to do this in a strange city; she also was uncertain of the exact date James would return. Therefore she reluctantly decided that since she had waited this long, she could wait a few more days.

Perhaps, she thought, he would be able to return earlier than he had promised. Her morale improved a little each day as the time of his expected arrival approached.

When nearly a week had gone by, she became very expectant. On the sixth day, she went to the place where the regular carriage from Paris arrived and waited for three hours for him. Arrival times for the carriage varied day by day depending on travel conditions. At last the carriage from Paris arrived. Looking anxiously at the passengers as they stepped out of the carriage, one by one, she soon realized that he was not arriving that day.

What a disappointment! On reflection though, she realized that she was being too impatient. After all, the week ended on the seventh day not the sixth.

She returned to the inn determined to cast out her feelings of disappointment. Taking up her sewing, she tried to keep busy so as not to dwell on her loneliness. Most of her days since James's departure were spent sewing and reading in their suite or taking long walks around town.

She was reluctant to develop any new friendships in the city because she was sensitive about her status as an unmarried woman living with a man in the inn, even though he was temporarily absent. She consoled herself thinking that, although she was terribly lonely, James would soon be with her and life would again be very pleasant. How eagerly she looked forward to his return.

On the seventh day, she again went to the carriage stop, this time full of anticipation that he would be arriving that day, just as he promised. She watched the passengers as they disembarked and, as the last one stepped out of the coach, she could not resist a small cry of dismay that he had not arrived. Bitterly disappointed, she returned disconsolately to the inn.

The next day she returned to the same place at the same time to wait for the incoming coach. He still did not arrive. Each day for two weeks she went through the same routine and each time felt more let down as he failed to appear. Her discouragement was palpable. The hours seemed longer with each passing day.

She worried that something bad may have happened to him. Was he having difficulty raising funds? Had robbers attacked the carriage? Could he have met with some accident in Paris? She inquired of carriage drivers and the innkeeper whether there had been any accidents or robberies recently along the route from Paris. None had occurred.

She thought of sending a letter to someone in Paris who might know how to reach James. Unfortunately, before he left he had mentioned only the first names of his friends, no last names. Nor had he told her any of the addresses of friends he hoped to visit. How she regretted that she had not obtained more details on his contacts in Paris! Anna had no friends of her own in Paris. There seemed to be no one in Paris she could contact by letter to inquire as to her lover's whereabouts.

When she was not worrying about his safety, sometimes Anna felt critical of James. Why did he not return when he said he would? Why had he not sent a letter of explaining his absence? How could he fail to look after her welfare in Amsterdam?

As the time lengthened and she saw her money dwindle, she had many other serious questions. Why wasn't he concerned about her financial circumstances when he left? Why did he not inquire whether she had sufficient funds? Why had he not made more effort to assist her financially during these many weeks?

At other times, she told herself that there must be some good reason why he did not return as planned, maybe he was involved in an accident or contracted a serious illness in Paris. Or perhaps he found himself in circumstances that made it impossible for him to send her a letter of explanation for his delayed return. Since he loved her so much there had to be a good reason. But what could it be? Thoughts of their great love sustained her.

Anna wrote a number of letters to James knowing, of course, that she could not send them to him because she had no address for him in Paris. Writing the letters provided her an outlet for venting her feelings during the long period of waiting for him to return. In some of her letters she poured out her great love for James. She also found that writing sonnets offered another satisfying means of expressing her thoughts of love and affection; she wrote a number of sonnets to James.

As time passed, the content of her letters changed. She became increasingly unhappy that she was left so long in Amsterdam without funds to cover her expenses and without any explanation for his failure to come back as promised. Her letters contained expressions of bitterness for his neglect. She retained all of her unsent letters in her personal belongings. She also retained love notes from James that he had passed to her personally from time to time in Copenhagen and Amsterdam.

At the beginning of the third week, Anna's funds became alarmingly low. After paying the innkeeper the rent, she only had money enough to pay for food and other necessities for a few days. With increasing anxiety, she continued to meet the daily carriage from Paris. She became more discouraged and worried each day as she found only disappointment at the carriage terminal.

Several more days passed and, despite every effort to conserve her limited funds, she finally had only money enough to buy bare necessities. Now she had to raise cash. There was only one possibility for doing so and that was to sell her jewels. Some of these jewels had been gifts from Bothwell and some from her parents. A few precious bracelets she had bought for herself.

She searched the city for a jeweler who would buy her precious items. When she finally found a dealer who offered her acceptable prices for her jewels, she sold them all. How difficult it was to part with her treasured jewelry! There were so many good memories, so much emotion, associated with these jewels. Yet she now had no choice but to sell them because her financial situation was desperate.

Having converted her jewelry to cash, she considered how best to use her only remaining resources. First, she set aside enough money to purchase passage on a ship that would take her back to Copenhagen. Would it actually come to that? How she dreaded the idea of returning to her parents in Copenhagen and explaining to them what had happened in Amsterdam. Nevertheless, she had to be realistic and regard a return to her parents home as a credible possibility.

The remaining money she would use for living expenses here. While deeply discouraged that James had not yet returned, nor had he even sent her a letter of explanation, she nonetheless still had some fading hope that he would return to her before her funds for living expenses were totally exhausted. Only if that happened would she leave Amsterdam.

With the funds now in hand for local expenses, she considered that she could afford to remain in Amsterdam only another week. Almost daily, she met the incoming carriage from Paris but with rapidly diminishing expectations. She returned to the inn each time further discouraged.

During that critical week she checked on commercial ships that were scheduled to depart for Copenhagen within days. She booked passage on one of them. The captain said she could pay for the passage when she came aboard to begin the journey two days hence. Having made this contingency plan, she returned to the inn full of despair. She was deeply troubled by the humiliation she would suffer if she returned to her parents home.

The following day she was too disconsolate to check the incoming carriage from Paris. Instead, she remained in her room and began the painful task of packing her trunk for the sad trip back to her home in Copenhagen.

It was nearly noon, when she heard a gentle knock on the door. Before she could walk over and open it, the door swung open and a cheerful James burst into the room! His arms held packages which he dropped to the floor so he could run over to hug and kiss her.

"How are you my darling? At last I'm back! Look, I have brought you presents," he said, picking them up from the floor and handing them to her.

Anna was speechless. She was shocked and at first felt a touch of resentment that he was so cheerful. Didn't he realize that he had left her in extremely difficult circumstances? His return was three weeks late and he had made no attempt to communicate with her. Now he had just burst into the room in a light hearted way as if he had been gone only a few days!

Soon, however, her negative feelings melted away and she felt the same strong attraction toward him that she had experienced earlier. His excitement was contagious and her total love for him returned. It was her nature to be loving and forgiving.

Before she could say anything, he tried to explain, "I am sorry for the long period of time you had to wait for me. It was necessary to stay longer in Paris than expected. I should have written to you but the time of my return was very uncertain. Each day I thought I could depart the following morning." She loved him so much she accepted all he said and could now forgive him for anything he had done or failed to do.

"I am so glad to see you!" She said and kissed him. "I was afraid some terrible accident or illness had occurred. I did not know how to reach you."

"Well, I did not know before my departure from Amsterdam where I would stay in Paris, so I could not give you my address there. Actually, I found an inexpensive inn and remained there the entire time. I had no luck contacting my friends but nonetheless had extremely good fortune in Paris."

"Did you see Mary Queen of Scots as you hoped to do?" she asked him.

"I did. Let me tell you about it," he said and briefly described the palace meeting with the queen. "My discussion with Mary Queen of Scots was quite useful. In particular, I received an important appointment from her and received assurances that she would have an undisclosed special assignment for me in the near future."

"I am so happy for you," Anna said as she hugged him. "Your future in Scotland is very bright indeed." She wondered how she fit into his new plans.

James did not inquire how Anna had spent these weeks alone in Amsterdam. He was so preoccupied with his own good fortune and career outlook that he did not stop and think about Anna's circumstances during the long period of his absence. As he continued to talk about his achievements and expectations, she was hurt by his failure to express concern for her during these past weeks. Nevertheless, she did not reveal how she felt.

"How long are we going to remain in Amsterdam?" she inquired, "And what are your plans for the next few days?"

"We will stay only a couple days here, dear," he replied.

"Will we be married here in Amsterdam as planned?" she asked, very well aware that their marriage had been deferred a very long time.

He was surprised that this delicate subject had arisen already.

"I have thought a lot about our wedding, darling," he answered, "and now I think it best that we wait until we are in Scotland. I want to stay here just long enough to arrange our passage on a ship to Edinburgh. I am now eager to return to my homeland as soon as possible. The queen may have need for my services very soon."

"I have waited a long time for the day of our wedding," she

said sadly, trying to hide her disappointment. "I guess I can wait a short while longer."

He was relieved that, however reluctantly, she agreed with him so readily on this sensitive point. He quickly changed the subject.

"There may not be many commercial ships sailing between Amsterdam and Scotland so it may take a day or two to arrange our passage. I'll begin this afternoon making inquiries about the arrangements. Until such booking can be made, let's enjoy ourselves as we did earlier. First, won't you open your presents?"

"Yes, darling," she said and began to open a small package. Ironically, it contained a beautiful jeweled necklace.

"How very pretty!" she exclaimed, not mentioning the fact that during his extended absence, she had been forced to sell all the jewelry she owned. "Thank you, sweetheart."

He helped her put on the necklace and admired her wearing it. She then opened two other gifts, perfume and a hat. She said, "thank you very much," and kissed him. She was pleased that he apparently had received enough money to buy these luxuries.

"Let's go downstairs and have a glass of wine before lunch to celebrate our reunion." James suggested.

They had the finest wine the restaurant could offer. Then they had a long, relaxed lunch of sole in the dining room.

In mid afternoon, James said, "This has been delightful but I must now search for a ship that can take us to Scotland."

"I'd like to go with you," Anna said. "I need to cancel a booking for a departure tomorrow. I was planning to return to Copenhagen."

James was surprised. "Why did you plan to leave?" he asked.

"Because I did not have the funds to remain in Amsterdam any longer," she replied candidly. "I lived as frugally as possible on my limited funds until they were exhausted. Then I sold all my jewelry and continued to stretch my funds as much as possible but they too vanished until all I had left was the cost of a trip back to Copenhagen."

"I am sorry. I did not realize you were in such financial difficulty, my darling," he said meekly. Then his usual exuberance returned as he assured her, "But now we have funds and can enjoy the rest of our time in Amsterdam!"

They walked together in silence to the nearest pier.

In a few days, James made arrangements for passage on a ship destined for Edinburgh. Anna was now delighted to be on her way to her new home in Scotland. While Amsterdam had been a scene of great pleasure for her it had also been a place of near despair and loneliness. She was glad to leave the city and optimistically contemplated her new life in Scotland with James.

CHAPTER 5

Living on James Estate in Scotland

James and Anna first caught sight of Scotland near Dunbar, along the south shore of the Firth of Forth. Both of them were excited to see the green hills of Bothwell's homeland. "Welcome to my beautiful Scotland, Anna," James exclaimed, clearly overjoyed.

With a gentle, favoring breeze, the ship soon turned westward and proceeded slowly up the Firth of Forth. They approached the port of Leith, near Edinburgh. The sails were trimmed and the ship glided gently into a berth.

After the ship was secured by lines to moorings on the pier and the gang plank was lowered, James and Anna quickly disembarked. Their trunks were off-loaded and James arranged for a carriage to take them to his home, Crichton Castle, eight miles south of Edinburgh.

"What a beautiful setting for the castle," Anna exclaimed, as she first saw the place at a distance. Crichton Castle was situated on a forest-covered hill.

"The original castle was built in the 14th century but it was later expanded," James explained.

An attractive courtyard surrounded the castle. A small cottage was located in a wooded area a short distance beyond the courtyard.

After the short carriage ride, they passed through a gateway and James said to Anna with obvious pride, "We are now actually on my estate. You now see my wonderful Chricton Castle at close range. How good it feels to be home again!"

"The castle is impressive," she acknowledged.

"There on the left is the cottage I described to you. I think we agreed that, for appearances sake, it would be preferable for you to stay for a time in the cottage rather than in the castle."

"Yes, I agree. The cottage is very quaint." The small, white cottage with a tile roof sat on a gentle slope. Many tall trees stood on three sides. One had a splendid view of the nearby mountains from the front of the house. The cottage was located only a five minute walk from the entrance to Crichton.

"Since the cottage is only a short stroll from the castle, it will be convenient for us to be together frequently," he said.

"Yes, of course, it is very close." Anna's unspoken thought, however, was that, although the cottage was very pretty and convenient, she did not want to stay there very long. She hoped that their living separately would be brief, that their long postponed marriage would soon be a reality.

"First, let us go to the castle and I will show you the living quarters." As the carriage neared the castle entrance, it's proud owner suggested, "I would like you to meet my household staff. You can call upon them for assistance anytime."

The carriage pulled up to the entrance and two servants came out to greet the earl: "It is nice to have you return, sir, after your long absence," one of the maids said to him.

"It is good to be back. This is my fiancee, Miss Anna Trondson. She will be living for a time in the cottage and I want you to go there immediately and see that everything is clean and in good order for her. In the meantime, we will rest awhile here."

"Yes, sir. The cottage will be made ready at once." The staff took James's trunks from the carriage and then the carriage proceeded toward the cottage with Anna's trunks. Meanwhile, James and Anna entered Crichton.

James guided Anna around the castle. While the rooms were sizable and well lighted, she was not entirely satisfied with some of the furnishings and thought about changes she would someday suggest. For now, however, she would keep her views to herself.

"The rooms are very attractive," she said.

After the tour of the castle, they rested for about an hour, sitting in a pretty flower garden on one side of the castle. They had drinks, and after a time, he suggested they walk over to the cottage. As they strolled along the path to the cottage, he pointed out a few other castles that could be observed far in the distance.

"I know the cottage is small but it is nicely furnished," he noted. "And you have a lovely view of the mountains to the south."

James opened the door and they entered the living room. She

cast her eyes about the room and then wandered through the small bedrooms and kitchen. She was pleased to see that her trunks were unopened in the bedroom; she preferred to unpack them herself.

"The cottage will be quite comfortable for me," she said. "And at any rate, it will only be for a short time."

"I will leave you to unpack your things and become accustomed to your new residence." He kissed her warmly and then returned to the castle.

Anna quickly adjusted to her new home. Nevertheless, she frequently wondered how long she would be living here rather than in the castle.

In the coming days, Anna said to herself, "I feel isolated at times, but it is a lovely spot." How she enjoyed the forest and streams of the estate! Often she walked long distances alone in the wooded area. Sometimes, James would join her on these walks, very much to her liking. For the first week, he was with her part of each day and evening.

After the first week James did not see her in the daytime but called on her every evening. He would remain until morning. The following week he saw her only a few times.

"I have not seen much of you in recent days," she observed when she next saw him.

"I have been unable to see you more often because there are so many things for me to do in Edinburgh and elsewhere these days. In particular, Queen Mary in Paris has authorized me and some other supporters to represent her in the new coalition Government of Scotland. I must attend many meetings."

Months passed and she became increasingly alone and concerned about setting the date when she and James would be married. "In Amsterdam," she recalled, "he assured me that we would be married 'soon' after we were settled in Scotland. What did he mean by soon?" she wondered. "Since he has not mentioned the subject recently, I must raise it with him again or he might continue to just let the matter drift. I dislike bringing up the subject once more as he seems uncomfortable when I raise it with him. Obviously, it would be so much better for him to initiate a discussion of the impending marriage but how long should I wait for him to do so?" Her patience was not inexhaustible.

During her third month in Scotland, James was visiting her in the cottage one evening. One subject dominated his thinking.

"The most astounding news has come from Paris," he said. "Young King Francis of France died recently and Queen Mary has decided to move to Edinburgh and rule Scotland, as is her right."

"That certainly is important news," she said. "How might this event affect you?"

James was very interested in speculating about the possible effects this dramatic change of circumstances meant for him. He was especially interested in considering how Mary's return to Scotland might affect his future.

"You may recall that when I talked with Queen Mary last August in Paris, she suggested that she might visit Scotland in the future and, in that case, would need an experienced seafaring man, such as myself, to serve as the escort for the queen and her entourage on the voyage to Scotland. Now, her situation has changed in such a way that she will not merely pay a visit here but will actually come to Scotland to take up residence and rule as queen. I may well be called in the near future to serve as her escort to Scotland," he boasted.

Anna was silent for a time, wondering whether he was again going to be absent from her for an extended period, as when he went to Paris and left her in Amsterdam. Then Anna gingerly raised a familiar issue.

"Darling, I hesitate to raise the subject again but have you given further thought to plans for our marriage?"

"For God's sake, why do you raise that matter now?" he exploded angrily. "Don't you realize that I am much too busy to arrange a wedding during this crisis in Government? How can I find time to think about a wedding? I expect at any time to be asked to go to France and escort Queen Mary to Scotland. This assignment will be a major responsibility and will require careful preparations on my part."

She was shocked at his outburst but remained silent.

He quickly cooled down somewhat and said, "You will just have to be patient until after this turmoil has ended."

She was disturbed by his loud, emotional response. After a few moments of silence, she spoke angrily. "You know very well that I have been very patient for a long time. There always seems to be some excuse for your delaying this important event. I am getting increasingly frustrated." She glared at him, and he looked aside.

James was surprised by her feisty reaction to his outburst and regretted that he had spoken in such an explosive way. He sought to quiet her.

"I know it has been difficult," he said soothingly. "You can be sure I will arrange it at the earliest possible time. Now, I must go to an important meeting." He kissed her quickly on her cheek and hurried away.

Anna stood still for a moment, bewildered by this emotional exchange, the first time he had shown any anger towards her. Although he got over it, once again Anna failed to get a definitive response from him on the date for their wedding. It was now months since James proposed to her in Copenhagen and assured her that they would be married in Amsterdam in July. She wondered if there would be more delays for one reason or another. Or had she, perhaps, finally been able to impress on him, through her own display of anger, the importance of avoiding further delay?

Bothwell's speculation that the queen might soon have need for his services in an important task, was prophetic. He was soon instructed to acquire the necessary ships on behalf of Queen Mary and prepare them suitably for transfer of the queen and her entourage from France to Scotland. August 1561 was the time set for the actual voyage transporting the queen to Scotland.

In carrying out preparations for this important task, Bothwell had to ascertain from authorities in the Edinburgh court the size of the queen's company and the amount of cargo that would be transported. He also needed the Navy to review its inventory of ships to determine which ones would be most suitable for the undertaking.

He discussed the matter first with various naval officers.

"I will need ships capable of eluding or countering attacks from enemies of the queen, particularly ships of the English navy," he told officers in charge of the records giving the characteristics of all the ships in the Scottish navy.

"We can readily identify a few ships that meet that requirement," they assured him.

"You realize that Queen Mary's ships must, if possible, be capable of sufficient speed to outpace enemy ships. The guns must have considerable firepower to defend the ships against attack."

"Yes, sir, we understand your needs," they assured him.

"One further point," the admiral stated, "If you find any deficiencies in the best ships you have available, I want to see the specifications for modifications you will undertake. You will need estimates of the amount of cargo to be transported. I will provide that information to you within three days."

"Aye, sir, you will have a complete report within two weeks."

Bothwell then went to the chamberlain of Holyroodhouse, the palace manager, with important questions concerning transport requirements.

"I will need a detailed list of the number of people, besides the queen, likely to be making the journey from France. In addition, I will need an estimate of the amount of goods that are likely to accompany the queen and her entourage. I will need this list within two days."

A few days later, he obtained the details concerning numbers of people and goods to be transported. Bothwell went back to the naval officials and presented this information to them. After lengthy discussions, Bothwell came to a basic conclusion.

"While the two or three naval ships you have identified have the necessary speed and defensive capability," he observed, "they lack the necessary cargo capacity required. Therefore, a large cargo ship in addition to strong naval ships will be necessary."

He made contacts with various commercial interests in an effort to lease or buy the cargo ship needed. There was not sufficient time to build a new ship for the planned voyage. The search for appropriate ships proved to be a time-consuming undertaking but they ultimately found a cargo ship suitable for the task.

"I want you to modify the cargo ship," Bothwell told naval officials, "by adding such weapons and defensive structures to the ship as required to enable it to cope with a possible attack."

"Aye, sir, it will be done as you order," they replied.

Many weeks were needed for procurement and modification of the ships for this major project. By June 1561, both ships were ready.

An important concern played on Bothwell's mind as he contemplated the operation. In July 1560, the Treaty of Edinburgh was agreed between Queen Elizabeth of England and representatives of Mary Queen of Scots and King Francis. The substance of the agreement was that Mary and Francis would no longer lay claim to the throne of England but recognize Elizabeth as the rightful Queen of England. The terms of the agreement were, however, never confirmed by Queen Mary and thus did not became official and binding. This thorny issue between Elizabeth and Mary continued to fester and adversely affect the royal relationships and international relations of the countries involved.

Prior to her departure, Queen Mary received a note, written by Queen Elizabeth, and delivered to her by the English ambassador to France.

The note read: "My dear Mary, I have received your request for a 'passport,' that is, a guarantee that the English navy will not interfere with the Scottish ships that will transport you shortly from France to Scotland. I am willing to issue the passport on condition that you first sign or ratify the Treaty of Edinburgh which officials in Scotland and England have already negotiated. As you know, this treaty includes a provision that states you disclaim any rights to the English throne. I await your reply. Elizabeth."

Queen Mary refused to sign the treaty before reaching Scotland because she intended to consult with her advisers there before acting on the treaty. Because of her refusal to sign the treaty in France, prior to the voyage, there was considerable risk that the English navy would interfere with this important voyage, at worst attacking her ships. Mary made it clear to all concerned that she would not agree to this treaty prior to her journey to Scotland. She decided to assume the risk of English interference with the voyage. Recognizing the risk, Bothwell and his crew felt there was a special need to prepare well for a possible English attack on the Scottish ships carrying Scotland's head of state.

Bothwell weighed various risks involved in the impending transfer of the queen to Scotland. He was concerned about the selection of the best route for the voyage in terms of avoiding interference by the English navy. Also, there was the consideration of selecting the optimum route from the standpoint of weather and sea conditions. The admiral decided the risks for the royal voyage would be reduced somewhat if he made a trial run of the sailing.

Early in the summer of 1561, his two ships were ready for the trial run. The captains and crews had been selected. He assembled the captains of two of the ships and their chief aides at the port of Leith and pointed out on a map the route to be taken from Leith to Calais, France. Admiral Bothwell described to the crew the risks involved in the voyage and how they planned to cope with them. He would be aboard the lead ship and have overall command responsibility for the small fleet. Once they reached Calais, instructions would be given as to the route they would take returning to Scotland.

One morning in July, the two ships proceeded out of the Firth of Forth on their trial-run voyage to Calais. About five days were required for the journey. No severe storms were encountered and generally the winds were favorable for sailing toward France. Bothwell and the captains were continuously on the alert for English ships. but none was encountered during the entire voyage. On arrival in Calais, they were greatly pleased that the first part of the trial run had been accomplished with so few problems.

On the return voyage of the trial run, the ships experienced worse weather than on the southbound journey, but the officers and crews were able to cope with the storms and high seas satisfactorily. Fortunately, they encountered no English war ships during the entire round trip.

"I suspect that the English navy knew this was a trial run and deliberately avoided interference with it," Bothwell speculated in the review of their experience with his subordinates.

"I feel sure that our crew took every precaution to keep our planned trial run a secret," the captain of one of the ships said.

"In any case, I consider the trial run a success," Bothwell told his officers and crew when the two ships finally reached Leith port. "The experience makes me confident that the impending royal voyage will be successful, too. With certain adjustments of the planned routes and arrangements for loading cargo in the ships, we should be ready for the major voyage."

When Bothwell was in France in June he had been in contact with a representative of the queen and the two of them reached an understanding that the queen would be ready to depart from Calais on the royal voyage in mid-August 1561. Thus the departure of Admiral Bothwell and his ships was timed, as closely as possible, so that they would arrive in Calais to meet the queen about the time she reached the port from Paris.

Admiral Bothwell's ships departed Leith in mid August following the same route chosen for the trial run. This time, however, a severe storm arose during the trip and two of the ships were severely battered and damaged by high seas. The damage greatly worried Bothwell but both ships were able to reach Calais. Since the ships arrived some days before the arrival of the queen, there was sufficient time to repair the damage to the two ships before her arrival.

Many carriages were required in Paris to transport Queen Mary, her group and their numerous trunks and other goods from Paris to Calais. Included among those in the carefully protected company were two of the queen's uncles, the Duke of Guise and the Cardinal of Lorraine. In addition, four maids and a poet were part of the company. On the route northward from Paris they stopped for rest first at Beauvais and then at Abbeville before finally reaching Calais port.

From one of his ships, Admiral Bothwell watched the arrival of the queen and the large amount of goods in the port.

"I am somewhat worried," Bothwell commented to his aide, "that this huge amount of cargo to be transported will exceed the capacity of our ships."

"It is certainly a large amount of cargo," his aide responded, "perhaps some of the lower priority goods can be shipped later on a commercial ship."

"I would be very reluctant to tell the queen that any of these goods cannot be accommodated on our voyage," the admiral said. "We simply must use the available space to maximum advantage and take it all."

In Calais, loading of the goods in the ships began immediately and all the goods were indeed squeezed in. Queen Mary and the others were forced to wait a few days in a Guise mansion until the weather for sailing was considered suitable. Then in late August, the royal group was ready to embark.

Bothwell left the ship and went to meet the queen.

"Bonjour, Monsier Bothwell. You are as good as your word. I am delighted to see you and the ships that will take us to Scotland."

"Bonjour, Your Highness. We are at your service, ready to escort you to your home."

"As soon as all passengers and remaining personal effects are transferred to the ships," he said, "we shall be on our way." Passengers wanted to be on deck as they left the port. Later, they could become settled in their quarters.

"Haul in the ship's mooring lines," Bothwell yelled. They were pulled aboard and the fleet departed from Calais.

The departure was a particularly emotional moment for Queen Mary who was leaving her beloved France where she had lived since she was a small child, some 13 years. She leaned over the railing of the lead ship as they proceeded seaward and quietly said goodbye to the land she loved so much.

Favorable winds carried the ships across the English Channel at a good pace. As they approached the English coast, three English naval ships loomed up ahead of them. They came close enough that their crews could be seen standing near the cannons on their decks clearly ready for action.

"Man the cannons," Bothwell ordered, "but hold your fire until I order it."

Flag signals were given from the lead ship to the captain of the cargo ship conveying the same orders.

"We shall wait until they fire the first shot," Bothwell said to his ship captain. "Meantime keep on a steady course northward. We will not be intimidated. If they attack, we will respond with full force." Bothwell kept to himself his concern that his ships would have a difficult fight if the English attacked since they had fire power superior to that of his three ships.

The menacing English warships continued to sail closely alongside the small Scottish fleet. They displayed the full array of their cannons which were aimed squarely at Bothwell's ships.

After threatening the Scottish ships for about an hour, the English warships suddenly veered off their course and departed. They took no action against the Scottish ships carrying the queen of Scotland even though the route of Bothwell's escort was fairly close to the English coast. The English obviously were well aware of the route of the Scottish ships but apparently decided to take no action against them.

After the threat had passed, Queen Mary came to the upper deck to talk with admiral Bothwell.

"That was a dangerous confrontation," she said to him.

"Yes it was, your highness. There was no way of knowing whether the English ships would attack," he replied.

"Apparently the intent was to threaten us, perhaps to prevent me from coming ashore. One thing is certain, Queen Elizabeth does not want me on English soil. She sees me as a major threat to her continued rule. Whatever their game, you handled the situation with excellent judgment in holding your fire until the threat ended and the fleet departed."

"Thank you, your highness. It is my duty to protect you at all costs."

Off the Yorkshire coast, the English fleet could have inflicted a major blow against Bothwell's ships. Perhaps the heavy mist that descended over the area made an armed engagement impossible. Maybe the English Government wanted only to prevent the queen from landing on English soil. Whatever the intent of the English, they abandoned their pursuit and the royal voyage now sailed safely toward the Firth of Forth.

Unlike the trip from Scotland to Calais, this operation toward Scotland encountered no major storms and, indeed, the weather during the five day journey was remarkably good. Before long, the ships carrying Queen Mary and her companions were secure in the relatively protected waters of the Firth of Forth. The three ships docked at the port of Leith, near Edinburgh, in the early morning hours.

"Welcome to Scotland Your Highness!" Bothwell said as she walked down the gang plank at the port of Leith. He had preceded her onto the pier so that he might be the first to greet her as she stepped onto her native Scotland. Queen Mary expected to be greeted by a guard of honor but instead was welcomed by only a few people as she disembarked.

"Why are there so few people here to greet me?" the queen asked Bothwell.

"The reason for the small gathering here is that your arrival was expected much later in the day. Let me conduct you to the home of a merchant for refreshment," Bothwell proposed. She nodded and Bothwell led the way.

"Welcome to Scotland, Your Majesty," Mr. MacEntire said as he ushered the queen into his home.

"Thank you," she replied somberly. "I am glad that you and a few other Scotsmen are here to welcome me to my homeland." It was apparent that she was not at all pleased that only a few people were in the port area to see her return to Scotland. Mr. MacEntire did his best to entertain the queen and her company in his home. A light meal was served along with wine. Then the guests were provided rooms for rest.

Although the hosts were friendly and respectful, Mary showed continued disappointment at the simple, quiet reception accorded her on her historic arrival in Scotland. How different the greeting would have been in France, she thought. When the group completed their rest, Mary noted that a light fog had formed over the area, enshrouding the town and adding to the somber atmosphere. The royal group was then escorted from the port to Edinburgh, a city of about 40,000 people.

Three streets dominated the general layout of Edinburgh. High street, Cowgate and Cannongate were more or less parallel. The High street was paved with stones, the other streets had only earth surface. A prominent building on the High street was the Old Tolbooth, a building used as a prison, a court building and sometimes the seat of Parliament. Along Canongate were houses of the nobles and behind them were gardens and fields. Some noble residences were also found on Cowgate. At right angles to the main streets were side streets on which poor houses, shops and some small gardens were located. Trash and filth was widespread. Each trade—goldsmiths, tinsmiths, butchers, etc.—had its own quarter. There was a busy central market. Market Cross was a place where proclamations were read and lawbreakers were put in pillories or hung on gallows. A tall ruined tower of Kirk o' Fields stood on open ground.

News of the queen's early arrival reached the city and quickly circulated about town. Soon a sizable group of townspeople gathered to welcome her as she entered the city. Also, a large number of officials and local dignitaries came to meet the arriving carriages, formally welcoming her to Scotland. Her spirits were raised somewhat by this greater show of welcome. Among the dignitaries was her half brother, Lord James of Moray, whom she had not seen for several years. Soon she was taken by Lord James and others to Holyroodhouse.

Mary could not help reflecting on the contrast between the sumptuous palaces of France and the relatively plain, even rustic, appearance of the Holyroodhouse palace she was now entering. In Paris, the principal palaces had rooms of utmost splendor, carpets of great beauty, grand mirrors at the end of halls, luxurious furniture, distinguished paintings and tapestries on the walls and impressive sculptures placed on pedestals about the salons. Here the interior of the palace was dark and somber. Furniture was utilitarian and uncomfortable. Few paintings and sculptures were to be seen. Floors lacked carpets.

"Let me tell you a little about the palace," said Lord James, Mary's half-brother and an important Protestant leader in Scotland. He escorted her to her apartments. She already knew a great deal about the famous royal house but she nevertheless let him to tell her about its history.

"As you can see," he began, "the Palace of Holyroodhouse is situated at the end of a road called Canongate; further west is the High Street that leads to Edinburgh Castle. The palace was constructed in the 12th century as a guest house for the nearby abbey founded by the Scottish King David I. The king built the abbey in 1128 in gratitude for the fact that his life was saved after a hunting accident. Immediately following the accident, he had a vision of the holy cross, or "rood." Thus the abbey was called, "The Church of the Holy Cross." In the course of time, the guest house, Holyroodhouse, became the principal palace of the royal families of Scotland."

"And where are my apartments?" she inquired somewhat impatiently.

"I shall show them to you in a moment," he replied. Then he continued, "A little more than a year has passed since the Regent Mary of Guise passed away," he related, as if she did not know the time of death of her own mother.

"Yes, yes," I know, she said with growing impatience.

Mary walked about the palace remembering good times she had spent here as a child before going to France. Although she would miss many of her friends and relatives in Paris, she was challenged by the problems she faced as Queen of Scotland. She knew, of course, that it would not be easy to accommodate the various clans and prickly leaders in this fractious society.

"Where can I have my mass?" she asked her brother as they walked from one room to another. Mary, as a deeply religious Catholic, was very concerned that she would have a suitable place for her worship services. James, a Protestant like the great majority of the people of Scotland, had little sympathy with her desire for a special room for Catholic mass.

"I'll show you a room you may use for that purpose," said James who was clearly troubled by the question. "I'd strongly suggest that you not flaunt your Catholic faith in Scotland because, as you know, the people are almost entirely Protestant and they have very little tolerance for the Papist faith."

She was infuriated by his impertinence, saying, "You know perfectly well that I came to Scotland with a clear understanding that I would be able to practice my Catholic faith without interference from anyone."

Lord James persisted. "Nevertheless, I strongly advise you to keep that practice as obscure as possible or you will invite severe criticism from Protestant leaders, leading noblemen and, indeed, the common people of Scotland. In the course of time, I suggest that you discuss religious practices with Reverend John Knox. Perhaps you will eventually see the wisdom of conforming to the religious views and practices of the people of Scotland."

Mary was furious at these suggestions. "I don't have the slightest intention of following the persuasions of John Knox. I'll only tolerate his views and he'll tolerate mine. And you had better not think I will change the Catholic beliefs I have held for many years."

"I know this contentious issue will also be a serious problem in your dealings with the leading nobles of Scotland. For now, all I ask is that you carefully avoid antagonizing influential nobles by discussing your Catholic views and practices."

"Just show me where I can hold my private masses," she said heatedly.

He led her to a small chapel that had been stripped of all Catholic symbols and decorations. It once had once been the room used for worship by her late mother. Mary said to herself that she would soon restore the chapel with proper furnishings. That would be one of her highest priorities.

"I will take care of the chapel," she said to her brother. With that crisp remark, they said goodbye and he left the room.

Earlier, while Queen Mary entered the port of Leith and was greeted by some local dignitaries, Anna stood silently in the small crowd, her eyes focused on James Hepburn. She, of course, was far more interested in his return to Scotland than the arrival of Queen Mary.

Although Anna was proud of the important assignment James Hepburn had undertaken in transporting the queen to Scotland, she was very lonesome as she had seen little of him in recent months. Her life these past weeks had been occupied by simple pleasures including sewing, tending her flower garden, and taking walks in the hills surrounding her cottage. In the evenings, especially, she missed the visits from James. She hoped that, with his important escort task now completed, she would see more of him. For the moment, however, she knew that Bothwell had to accompany the queen from the port to the palace, and it was clearly impossible to approach him under these circumstances.

As the queen's escort group, including Bothwell, departed the port area and the local population dispersed, returning to their homes or places of work, Anna slowly made her way alone to the horse and carriage that would take her back to the cottage near Crichton Castle. On the ride from Leith, she again reflected that it had now been over a year since she left Denmark and wondered what the future held for her. Would James now have more time to spend with her? Would he finally take the time to arrange for their marriage?

Her carriage pulled up beside the cottage and she disembarked. She entered her small house with a feeling of sadness. Why, she asked herself, was she feeling so sad when her lover had just returned to Scotland? Shouldn't she be rejoicing at his return? The problem was that she could not be with him now, and she feared he would again find diversions that would often keep them apart.

As if to confirm these fears, she looked out the cottage window and saw that James was returning to Chricton and went directly into the castle, not stopping to see her after his long absence. She knew instinctively that it would be a mistake for her to rush over to see him. But how long would it be before he come to see her?

After a couple weeks during which James did not come to her cottage, Anna confronted him one day as she walked by the front door of the castle.

"I haven't seen much of you lately," she said coolly.

"Yes, I know. Problems in the Parliament have kept me very busy," he replied.

"During the daytime, yes, but I often see you entering your castle in the early evening, "she said testily.

"Have you been spying on me then?" James said, raising his voice.

"I wouldn't call it spying but I happened to see you and your old girl friend, Bessie, arrive here on three occasions and I am sure she was not visiting to have tea with you."

"All right, damn it! So what if I spend an occasional evening with an old friend," he stormed.

"I know we aren't married and therefore, in a sense, you might regard yourself as a free man," she replied quietly, "but we have a basic relationship and you have promised to marry me." She wiped a tear with her handkerchief.

"I know, I know," he cooled down. He regretted that he caused her to return again to that familiar theme. "Bessie will not return, so don't worry."

"I hope not," Anna replied and hurried to her cottage.

CHAPTER 6

James Lands in Prison

The demands on Bothwell's time were only slightly reduced after Queen Mary was safely installed in Holyroodhouse Palace in Edinburgh. To demonstrate the confidence she had in his ability and loyalty, she appointed him a member of the Privy Council. He was one of twelve members of the Council. This new responsibility imposed on him duties both to attend formal meetings of the Privy Council and to participate in many other less formal meetings. The Council meetings were often full of rancor between contentious nobles, and Queen Mary tried very hard to bring about some reconciliation of differing views, with limited success. She found it hard to understand their capacity for hatred.

The queen appointed Bothwell Lieutenant of the Borders, and he departed immediately to quell disturbances among the pugnacious people in that area. Since Bothwell was a resident of the Borders he knew many of the people in this territory well. As Lieutenant of the Borders he now had the authority to keep the peace here.

During the daytime he was generally in Edinburgh or traveling around the Borders in an effort to resolve disputes. Despite these new duties, however, James seemed to find more time to see Anna, to her great pleasure. For a while, he spent many evenings with her in the small cottage near Crichton Castle. Although she resented his absences and had doubts about his love during those times, she could not resist him when he came to her. Her love for him, though variable, remained overpowering.

One evening, Anna vaguely hinted again at her desire to have him plan their wedding. She had learned from past conversations to speak cautiously on the subject. If she raised it directly, he would stiffen somewhat and become less congenial. He also seemed to come to her cottage less often for a time after she raised the subject. These reactions made her reluctant to bring up the issue directly.

"I heard a rumor from your household staff that your sister, Lady Janet Hepburn, will soon marry Lord John Stewart, one of the queen's half brothers," she said quietly.

"Yes, they will be married at Crichton in January," he replied. "I shall have much to do in preparation for my sister's wedding."

He made no mention of any marriage involving himself and Anna.

"You are, of course, invited to attend the wedding," he added before changing the subject.

"I must return to Holyroodhouse for a meeting of the Privy Council," he stated and rose abruptly to take his leave of her. They embraced quickly, and he departed as she stood wistfully by the open door.

During the month of January, as planned, the wedding of Lady Janet and Lord John was held at Crichton. It was a grand affair with much feasting on various kinds of game including deer, elk, pheasant, and pig. Also, sports entertained the guests on the castle grounds, particularly jousting. Many people attended the splendid event, including the queen and various members of her court. Among them was the queen's brother, Lord James, the Earl of Moray. With Lord James was his fiancee, Lady Agnes Keith, with whom he was to be married the following month.

Anna joined the throng for a time. She did not feel comfortable in that setting, however, since James Bothwell was preoccupied as a host and as a member of the wedding party. Thus he was unable to spend time with Anna during the reception and entertainment. While the guests danced happily, Anna quietly slipped away and went to her cottage. How she wished this could have been her own wedding!

One of the members of the court who attended the wedding was the Earl of Arran, a close relative of the queen. Arran was generally regarded in the community as unstable, even a little crazy. As a near relative of Queen Mary, however, his peculiar ways were generally tolerated. During the dance, a drunken Arran roughly shoved the groom away from his new bride and briefly attempted to dance with her in a wild, uncontrolled fashion. The bride and groom were very embarrassed. Bothwell was upset by the antics of Arran during his sister's wedding and vowed to get even with him for these disturbances.

Some weeks later, Bothwell's chance for reprisal against Arran came when he, Lord John Stewart (the queen's half-brother), and the queen's uncle Rene Elboeuf decided to embarrass Earl Arran. The opportunity arose when the three men discovered one evening that Arran was with a prostitute. Bothwell and Elboeuf forced their way into the home, surprising and embarrassing the naked Arran.

Earl Arran complained about the incident to the queen, who was disturbed by the behavior of Bothwell and Elboeuf. Arran persuaded the queen that his girl friend was not a prostitute. Moreover, the Protestant church forcefully criticized the Catholic Elboeuf for his participation in the incident. Queen Mary issued a strong rebuke to both Bothwell and Elbouef for their participation in the affair.

The three men, Bothwell, Elboeuf and Lord John, brushed off the criticism. They considered their interference in Arran's affair merely a harmless prank. In fact, they threatened to repeat the boisterous affair the next night. Before they could carry out the escapade again, however, the three were persuaded by friends to disperse. Soon thereafter, Arran and Bothwell were seemingly reconciled, thanks to the intervention of John Knox, but the negotiated peace between the two prominent men did not last long.

John Knox, as the strong-willed leader of the Scottish Reformation, set an austere moral tone for the Protestant Church of Scotland. The tempestuous Knox had been agitated by the horrific action of the Catholic Cardinal David Beaton in burning a prominent Protestant leader, George Wishart, for heresy in 1546.

After that event, Knox was determined to eliminate any practice of Catholicism in Scotland.

Lord James Stewart, the half-brother of Queen Mary, was a good friend and close political ally of John Knox. They shared a common belief in the Church of Scotland. In contrast, Mary as a fervent Catholic differed strongly with Knox and from time to time they got into heated arguments. Knox tried many times to convert the Roman Catholic Mary Queen of Scots to the Protestant faith but without success. He was a frequent critic of Queen Mary not only in meetings with her but also in his impassioned sermons from the pulpit of St. Giles Church in Edinburgh. Politics and religion were intertwined in Scotland, political alignments being heavily influenced by religious differences.

In a third incident involving Bothwell and Arran, the unstable nobleman spread a story throughout the Edinburgh community that Bothwell suggested the two of them join in a conspiracy to abduct the queen and seize political power in Scotland. Arran stated this charge in a letter to the queen in March 1562, giving a full description of Bothwell's alleged proposal. He sent the letter to both Queen Mary and Lord James.

This particular charge was considered so serious and sensitive that it could not be viewed by the queen and her government as a mere practical joke. The charge was treated by the authorities as a real threat to the throne by Bothwell, a leading member of the queen's court.

On the basis of Arran's letter, Bothwell was immediately arrested for conspiracy. A meeting of the Privy Council was convened and Bothwell was charged in that proceeding with a high crime. The Council judged him guilty of treason. A prominent member of Privy Council reviewing the case was Lord James who had never been friendly to the Earl of Bothwell. No trial was deemed necessary, and Bothwell's imprisonment was ordered even though it was well known that Arran had reason to carry out a reprisal against Bothwell for the earlier embarrassment caused Arran.

On the other hand, it is possible that the impulsive Bothwell, who often did not weigh carefully the consequences of his actions or words, made some remark in jest about abducting the queen. Arran could have taken such a remark seriously and then elaborated on it to his own advantage.

Lord James had long held a very low opinion of Bothwell and firmly opposed a court proceeding on the basis that a public trial of Bothwell would be politically very embarrassing to the queen. Lord James feared that a public trial would probably reveal that Arran had lied in making the abduction charge. Since Earl Arran was a near relative of the queen, such a revelation to the general public would be intolerable, as it would reflect adversely on the royal family.

Queen Mary was actually inclined to have a public trial but Lord James was able to persuade her that it would be unwise, clearly against her own interest. Thus Bothwell, denied a trial, was quietly placed in a prison cell in Edinburgh Castle without further legal proceeding. Protestations on his part fell on deaf ears.

Edinburgh Castle, located about a mile west of Holyroodhouse, was constructed high on a crag of volcanic rock. There are steep cliffs on three sides; on the fourth side there is a ramp that extends from the castle down to level ground. A kind of fortress occupied this Edinburgh site as early as the 13th century. Part of the fortress on the site was built in the 11th century. Countless battles were fought at this location over the centuries. St. Margaret's Chapel was the only building remaining when the English forces defeated the Scots here in 1313. Following that defeat, new structures were built on the impressive promontory. The prison in the castle was situated so that escape of a prisoner from the castle was considered impossible. The queen and the Privy Council therefore felt assured that Bothwell was securely removed from the outside world.

Sitting in his prison cell, Bothwell had ample time to contemplate recent events that led to his imprisonment. How did he fall so quickly from the heights of power and influence to such a low and unfortunate state? He had held an enviable position as a member of the queen's Privy Council and the royal court. He had access to great wealth. Now he was deprived of all of those benefits and placed in a prison. In his confinement, he could do nothing toward restoring himself to his former status.

Why had he gone after Arran so recklessly, allowing his passions to get the better of his reason? Why did he goad Arran into making those wild charges?

Bothwell had no good answers to these and other troubling questions. He vowed that if he ever again had a chance to reach a high position he would act with more deliberation and rationality. For now, the prospects of such a second chance seemed dim indeed. He was depressed. The earl languished for months in Edinburgh prison. Escape seemed impossible.

He was confined to a small cell with a single window to the open air. The window had iron bars to prevent escape. A bed, table and chair were the only furnishings provided in the cell. He was allowed to have books and several volumes he requested were supplied to him. Reading these books helped him enormously to keep his mind occupied during the countless long days. He was also allowed some writing paper, ink and a pen and was permitted to send letters outside the prison.

An alarmed Anna, learning about his incarceration, attempted to visit him in the prison. She requested, on several occasions, permission to visit him, but all these requests were denied. She was very disappointed but found no one who could overrule the authorities on the matter. Evidently, the Government wanted to prevent any direct contact between anyone in Edinburgh and Bothwell in prison.

Anna was allowed, however, to send letters to James while he was in prison. She wrote several impassioned letters to him, proclaiming her love for him and telling of her longing for his release from prison. She even wrote some poetry in which she expressed her strong feelings of love for him.

In return, James wrote letters to her in which he also expressed his love for her. He promised once again that they would be married after he obtained his release from prison, which he hoped would be soon. His letters included emotional pleas that she seek help from various of his friends who might assist in obtaining his freedom. The letters included specific suggestions as to useful arguments and approaches to employ in these efforts. He also spared her no details on the poor conditions in which he was confined. One might well doubt the sincerity of James professions of his love for Anna, given the aggressive manner in which he solicited her assistance in exploring ways to secure his release from prison. These letters would be featured in a surprising situation a few years later.

Despite Anna's attempts to obtain James release, the government persisted in its rigid position that he be held in Edinburgh Castle indefinitely. Discouraged by Anna's lack of success in efforts to help him, James conceived a risky plan to escape from the hated prison, a plan that involved bribing the prison guard who regularly brought meals to him. But how amenable would the guard be to cooperation? Through carefully developed conversations with the guard over a period of time, perhaps he could obtain cooperation.

One evening as the guard brought his meal, Bothwell began a conversation with him designed to test the man's willingness to cooperate in an escape plan.

"How long have you worked in the prison?" he asked casually.

"More than five years," the guard replied.

"Do they pay you well?

"Not enough."

"Why not enough? You must be paid as well as most prison employees."

"I am paid as well as other guards and I can't really expect them to pay me more than the others, but my house and much of my furniture were destroyed by a fire last month. I have found a house to rent but the rent is high and I don't have money to buy furniture."

"Suppose someone would make it possible for you to actually buy a house and also furniture."

The guard hesitated before answering. Then he replied, "That would never happen. No one would do such a thing for me." He stood near the door and did not leave. He wanted to hear more.

Bothwell studied the man carefully, trying to read his mind. The guard weighed the germ of an idea that was now planted in the his mind. The prisoner realized, of course, that there was a significant risk that the guard might report an attempt to bribe him. Such a report could lead to worse treatment for Bothwell, perhaps torture or even execution. But what options did he have? Shrugging off that risk, the prisoner decided to take the chance.

"I think you know that I am an earl and an admiral with a sizable estate and considerable wealth. Therefore, I am in a position to provide you with the funds you need to buy a house and furniture for your family."

The guard remained standing by the cell door, nervous and fearful. If he reported to the head of the guards this attempted bribery he would probably be rewarded financially. But how much would that be? Rather little, he concluded.

"If you helped me take care of my financial problem what would you expect me to do for you?"

Bothwell breathed a sigh of relief. The man was vulnerable as expected. "Simply bring me a good file with my meal tomorrow night. That is all." The prisoner had studied the bars on his cell and knew he could cut them with a file. While his cell window was high above ground level, he sensed that he could tolerate the drop from the window to the ground without injury. Thus all he needed to make his escape was a file to cut the bars in the cell window.

"I could bring the file but how could I be assured that you would carry out your side of the bargain?" the guard asked apprehensively. "How can you pay me here since you have nothing? So how do I know you will pay me?"

"You will have to trust me as a man of honor. I will give you a note that you can take to a close friend of mine instructing him to pay you, on my behalf, two hundred pounds sterling in cash. That should be sufficient to cover your purchases."

The guard stood quietly for a time, wondering whether he could trust the prisoner to make good this payment. Although he knew there was considerable risk that he might be caught or not receive the money, he decided this was an opportunity of a lifetime, a chance to gain a small fortune. As he left the cell, the guard said simply, "All right, I will bring it tomorrow night."

Bothwell was elated. There was no doubt in his mind that the plan would work.

The next evening, the guard brought him the usual meal and set it down on the table. Then he withdrew a file from his coat pocket and handed it to Bothwell. "I hope you realize the risk I am taking. I could be severely punished, even lose my life, for providing this file," the guard said with obvious concern.

"We are both taking risks," Bothwell replied, "but we both have much to gain as well." In exchange for the file, the prisoner gave the guard a note addressed to a friend, instructing him to make the agreed payment. The guard quietly withdrew and locked the cell door. He realized that, after the escape, he would have to explain to the captain of the guard why he could not have been the one providing the prisoner with the file. He knew that two visitors had been in Bothwell's cell during the past month. He could implicate them. In any case, the captain would have no proof that the guard had brought the file to the prisoner.

The guard also contemplated that a successful escape from the prison was highly unlikely. If Bothwell died in the attempted escape, prison authorities would not be greatly concerned about the means used by the prisoner to break out of his cell. In the meantime, the guard would obtain the money promised him.

During the night, Bothwell worked vigorously cutting the bars of his cell. By early morning, while it was still dark, he had made a large enough space to squeeze through. Bothwell crawled through this space and perched outside the cell window on the thick wall's ledge. Because of the darkness, he could not see the ground, but he had studied the situation carefully during the day and knew roughly what to expect when he hit the ground. Nevertheless, he felt apprehensive of what he might really encounter in his fall.

He first tied some of his clothing to a cell bar and held onto the other end. With only a slight moonlight to reveal the ground below, he slowly worked himself down the string of clothes as far as possible. It was still a long way to the rugged hillside below. He hesitated before releasing his grip, again wondering how he would hit the ground. His heart was pounding and his strength was ebbing. Finally, he had to let go and was in free fall. He hit the ground feet first and rolled over in the weeds. He felt a tremendous relief. Although he ached from the heavy fall, he was still intact, no broken bones. A few minutes rest renewed his energy.

He then walked along the narrow edge of the cliff, hugging the outer wall of the castle and gradually found his way to a steep slope on which he scrambled down to lower elevation. Slowly, he walked and stumbled downward to a more gentle slope and finally to the level ground. The escape from the castle was a severe challenge but he did it and he felt a great release from the tension felt during the precarious descent from his cell window in the darkness. He had survived escape from Edinburgh. Would he be able to avoid capture elsewhere in Scotland?

While it was still dark with only an occasional faint light from the moon, he stealthily moved through the town until he came to the home of a trusted friend. He knocked on the door and waited for an answer.

A voice yelled at him through the door, "How dare you bother me during the middle of the night! Go away."

Bothwell replied, "John, I need your help. Let me in."

John Rhodes recognized with amazement the voice of his friend and opened the door. "I thought you were in prison. When did they release you? Why are you coming to my place in the middle of the night?"

"You ask many questions and I do not have time to give you long answers. I am out of prison and on my way to the Borders but I need some help."

"What do you need? Maybe I can help. But I do not want to get in trouble with the authorities."

"All I need from you are two things: a horse and enough money to obtain passage on a ship to some European port."

"I only have one horse at present and I guess I can do without him awhile. Would ten pounds sterling be enough money? That is all I have in the house. I can let you have that amount."

"Yes, that would be enough. Please hurry, John. I must be on my way quickly."

John rushed to his bedroom and found the hidden money. Then he took Bothwell to the barn behind his house and they found the horse.

As Bothwell got on the horse, John asked, "You didn't tell me how you obtained your release from prison. How did it happen?"

"I will explain it all to you when I return some day to repay you for your help. Thanks and goodbye." He hurried away into the darkness.

He rode for a couple of hours and finally stopped at the cottage of his good friend, Janet Beaton, in the Borders area.

Janet Beaton was married, had several children and was nearly twice the age of Bothwell. The slim, pretty Janet came from a respectable family, one of her close relatives being a high official of the Catholic church. She and Bothwell had a brief, impassioned fling some years earlier. Their friendship continued friendly but not serious.

"What are you doing here?" She exclaimed as she opened the door and let him into her house. "I thought you were in prison."

"Well, as you can plainly see, I'm not in prison. I just left Edinburgh Castle."

"And how did you leave?" she asked. She wondered whether he could possibly have escaped from that incredibly secure prison.

"Let's say someone allowed me to leave." Bothwell replied ambiguously. Changing the subject somewhat he said, "Janet, I have been traveling for some hours and I am very tired. Is it all right with you if I rest here for awhile?"

Is anyone coming after you who will give me trouble for letting you stay here?"

"There is no danger of that. None of my enemies know where I am and at any rate, they will not start looking for me until a few hours from now."

"All right, rest a while."

He rested in her home for a few hours. While he was sleeping, Janet searched her closet and found some men's clothing. After he awoke she gave him the clothes and he put them on.

As he departed on his borrowed horse, Bothwell waved

goodbye to Janet. "Thank you for your help, Janet. I will remember it."

Bothwell rode to the nearby port of Berwick and located a ship with a French flag. He learned that the ship was soon to leave for France.

"Can you take me to France?" he asked the ship's captain.

"Yes, if you can pay for your passage," the captain replied. "We leave for Calais early in the morning. You can come aboard now if you wish. I have a cabin free."

He paid the captain and was directed to his cabin. Here he waited impatiently for the ship to leave port. He could not sleep. But no one came looking for him and as the sun was rising the ship departed. Bothwell at last could relax a little.

As the ship proceeded southward off the coast of northern England, a violent storm arose and the ship soon was in serious trouble.

"Why don't you change your course so you sail directly into the wind?" Bothwell yelled at the captain. "Your ship cannot take these powerful blows from the east, "I can handle it," the captain replied confidently. "We can escape the storm shortly if we proceed southward. The storm cannot last much longer."

Bothwell was skeptical. He had experienced similar storms in this area and knew they could be severe.

Before long, the old ship was groaning from the strain on its hull. The rigging became a mess of tangled sail and a broken mast. As the ship threatened to break apart, the captain succeeded in directing it into shallow water. Here it came to rest on the sea bottom. Huge waves rolled over the ship causing it to break up. The captain and crew desperately sought to save themselves by grabbing flotsam or attempting to swim ashore.

"I told the old fool to reorient his ship to save it," Bothwell said to himself as he clung to a remaining mast on the ship. "Now I see no chance to save it."

Bothwell fled the doomed ship, swimming as best he could through the violent waters until he reached water shallow enough that he could walk through the crashing surf to safety. He stumbled ashore and soon fell exhausted on the beach. Here he rested for a brief time, but the cold soon forced him to get up and push further inland.

He wondered whether he was in England or Scotland. There was no way to tell. As he walked from the beach, his way was lit only by occasional flashes of lightning. The terrain was familiar to him as, over the years, he had participated in many skirmishes between Scots and Englishmen in this territory. He guessed that he was in England but probably not far from the border between Scotland and England. Was he near enough to the border, he wondered, to cross into Scotland?

Struggling through the rough fields and ceaseless rain, he was able to reach a cluster of houses. He then recognized the place and knew for certain that he was in England. He could hardly believe his luck when he found a house that belonged to an English acquaintance,

The people who lived in this area were generally bitter enemies of the Scottish people, particularly the Scots of the Borders area of Scotland. But George Thomas, who lived in this house, was one of a very few Englishmen whom Bothwell regarded as somewhat friendly. Bothwell had actually saved the life of this farmer once during a skirmish when he was about to be killed by Scots. Bothwell prevented the slaying because Thomas had once returned stolen cattle to his estate.

"Who are you?" the man inside yelled.

"I am the Earl of Bothwell," he replied. "I have been ship-wrecked just offshore. I need shelter."

George Thomas slowly opened the door and let Bothwell into his house. "My friend, you are welcome! The weather is miserable. Get inside"

Bothwell entered shivering from cold, water dripping from his clothes and face. "Thanks!"

"Come near the fire. It's a stormy night. You must be very cold." George put a log on the dimly glowing embers to give more warmth in the room.

When his guest stopped shivering and was able to talk about

his plight, George asked, "What happened to you out there? I know you wouldn't be in this English territory unless something serious happened."

"I was aboard a French ship sailing from Scotland to France and the ship broke apart in the storm and floundered into shallow water. With a great deal of difficulty I was able to reach the shore."

"What a terrible experience! You are lucky to be alive."

"You are right. I fear that most of the others on the ship did not make it. I saw no one else on the beach as I left it and walked inland."

"Where will you go from here?" George asked anxiously, "You know you have many enemies on this side of the border. It is not safe for you to stay in this area. In fact, I would be in considerable trouble with my neighbors if they found out I sheltered you. I expect you will want to go back to your home in the Borders as soon as possible."

"Actually, my enemies in Scotland are aggressively searching for me at this moment, so I cannot return to Scotland quite yet."

George pondered that statement and then said, "Well, let us both get some rest tonight and discuss the problem early in the morning. I suggest you leave the house before daybreak."

The following morning, the two men agreed that Bothwell should leave his friend before dawn and make his way as best he could through the hostile country to the nearest port where the Scottish earl might be fortunate enough to find another ship and escape undetected from England to the continent.

While still dark, Bothwell quietly left his friend's house riding on a horse George let him take. He followed a dirt road George had described to him. It led toward a nearby small port. It was difficult to see his way in the darkness with only a faint moonlight occasionally showing through the clouds. The darkness was good, he thought, as he would not likely be observed by any local people who might be about this early. He tried to follow the roadside markers in the darkness.

Despite his efforts to avoid being observed, a small group of men on horseback suddenly appeared before him. For a moment, he considered galloping away but doubted his old horse could outpace these riders if they chose to pursue him. Perhaps he could talk his way free.

"Who goes there?" one of them asked in a somewhat friendly voice.

"Just a traveler," Bothwell replied. He did not want to engage in a conversation and continued to ride at an even pace along the road.

"Wait a minute!" one of them said. "Do you live in this area?"

Bothwell did not answer but continued to ride onward hoping they would leave him alone. But the men rode up to him and one of them said, "You sound like a Scotsman! Where are you from?"

"I told you I am just a traveler. Please let me be on my way."

"I think you better come with us. We like to know who is in our area, especially if he is a Scotsman." They were three strong men and Bothwell knew it was useless to resist them. They brought him to the local magistrate in a nearby small town.

Since it was very early in the morning, the magistrate did not wish to deal with the man until later in the day. Bothwell was held in custody and told that his case would be handled by higher authorities in the morning.

The following day, the authorities found reason to postpone a hearing on the case and he was simply held in the local jail. Someone recognized him and Bothwell knew they would deal with him harshly. Within a few days, Bothwell was sent to a local prison without a trial. There was reason enough to hold him given that the Scotsman had entered England without permission.

Bothwell was held in the prison in northern England for several months while local officials deliberated at leisure what to do with him. They were in no hurry to release the troublesome Scottish Borderer.

While in prison, Bothwell wrote a letter to Queen Elizabeth explaining his unjustified retention and requesting that she intervene and have him released. The English queen had excellent sources of intelligence on Scottish affairs. Unfortunately for Bothwell, the queen knew very well of Bothwell's close association with her cousin Queen Mary as well as the incident with Earl Arran that led to Bothwell's imprisonment.

Queen Elizabeth had also learned about Bothwell's daring escape from Edinburgh prison and knew that he was being pursued by his enemies in Scotland. Her agents in Edinburgh reported that John Knox had a different take on how Bothwell obtained his freedom. The outspoken minister in Edinburgh charged in a sermon at St. Giles Church that Bothwell had actually obtained "easy passage at the gate of Edinburgh," implying that Queen Mary had allowed him to go free. Knox seldom missed an opportunity to criticize the Catholic queen.

The English queen felt it important that Bothwell be brought to London for talks. She thought such discussions would provide valuable intelligence which might prove useful in her dealings with the Scottish Government. Therefore, she asked that he be transferred from the prison in northern England to the Tower of London. From there, she could summon him to the palace at her own convenience for interviews.

When Bothwell was informed that he would be moved to the Tower of London he was somewhat encouraged. Since he would then be near the center of power in England, his case would be heard at the highest level of government. He was confident that, if given an opportunity to explain his situation, he would be released from prison in England and could continue his interrupted travel to France. He could see no reason for English authorities to hold him.

Soon, he was taken to London and placed in the Tower. He convinced himself that he would be able to persuade Queen Elizabeth that he should be released.

Weeks passed without Bothwell being summoned to the palace. This delay was very discouraging. He became impatient for an opportunity to plead his case. Then one day, without forewarning, he was escorted to the palace and brought into the presence of Queen Elizabeth.

She addressed him, saying "I understand that you entered England without permission some months ago and that you recently asked to meet with me to explain why you should be allowed to go free."

"Your highness, you are right that I entered your country without permission, but I did not come to England voluntarily. The ship on which I was traveling was destined for France but was wrecked in a violent storm off the coast of England and I barely escaped with my life to the English shore."

"Why did you not return to Scotland immediately?" she asked. She knew perfectly well why he did not return to Scotland but wanted to hear his explanation.

"Because my enemies in Scotland would return me to the Edinburgh prison from which I escaped."

"Do your Scottish enemies include the government of Queen Mary?"

"Yes," he replied with candor, "Lord James of Moray convinced the queen that I was a danger to her. In fact, I am not a danger to her at all. As you know, I escorted her from France to Scotland two years ago."

"I am aware of the service you performed to Queen Mary. Lord James is a dangerous man and I fear he is determined to take control of the throne of Scotland from Queen Mary." The queen hesitated, frowned and raised her voice, asking "Do you intend to return to Scotland?"

"Under present circumstances, I do not wish to return to Scotland. I was imprisoned unfairly. If I could be assured of a fair trial in Edinburgh I would be glad to return there. I realize that I broke the law by escaping from a royal prison, and I would like to clear my name. My imprisonment was entirely without justification but was engineered by my enemies, particularly Lord James. The queen took his advice that I should be sent to Edinburgh prison. As long as Queen Mary listens to his advice, I cannot be confident of a fair trial. Therefore, I plan to go to France," he explained. As I told you, I was bound for France when I was ship-wrecked in northern England. I still want to go to France and live for a time."

"Is it your intention to abandon Scotland forever?"

"No, indeed not," he replied quickly, "I shall return when

conditions become more favorable for me. When Queen Mary is independent of her brother's influence, I'll be back in my homeland."

"You will be interested to know that Lord James has written to me urging that I not return you to Scotland but that I dispose of you as I see fit."

"I am not at all surprised that he has made that statement. He fears that if I return to Scotland, I will be a continuing threat to him as counselor to the queen, giving her different advice than he gives her," Bothwell replied.

"I see no reason for you to be detained in England further. You are free to go to France as soon as you wish to do so." She signaled that the interview was closed.

"Thank you your highness!" He bowed deeply as he retreated from the room. Bothwell was elated.

He soon sailed to Calais, France, and traveled by carriage to Paris. Here he contacted an influential uncle of Mary Queen of Scots, Charles, Cardinal of Lorraine, who had a strong interest in Scotland, particularly the Catholic church of Scotland.

"Sir," Bothwell began, "I think you already know much about my unfortunate experiences during the past two years, both in Scotland and in England. Nevertheless, I can assure you of my absolute loyalty to Scotland, and despite her attitude toward me, my loyalty to the queen."

"I am pleased to hear you say that," the Cardinal replied. "The queen has had a difficult time because of the strong opposition from aggressive Protestant leaders, especially Lord James."

Bothwell agreed, "I have contended with Lord James on numerous occasions and am aware that he is an unhelpful counselor to the queen. He persistently opposes her adherence to her Catholic faith."

"I am well informed on that subject and wish something could be done to bring about greater religious tolerance in Scotland."

The admiral failed to tell the Cardinal that he had no deep convictions on religion. He was pragmatic. He sided with Protestants or Catholics, depending on who best served his ambitions for advancement. "Though a Protestant, I for one can assure you that I favor tolerance of different faiths in my native land," Bothwell said at this point.

"I appreciate that attitude and I am sure Mary is aware of your views on this subject, the Cardinal commented. "Now, what can I do for you?" he asked.

"Perhaps you can be helpful to me in securing a position with the Scottish Guard in Paris," Bothwell suggested. "It is not timely now for me to return to Scotland, as you recognize, and I need some source of income while I remain in Paris."

"Your request comes at a most favorable time," the Cardinal observed, "because the position of Captain of the guard is currently open. I'll talk with the ambassador about the matter and let you know what is decided." Within a week, Bothwell was notified by the Cardinal that his appointment had been approved. The news was most welcome as it assured him of a satisfactory income for an indefinite period.

Shortly before Bothwell's imprisonment at Edinburgh, Anna found cause for joy. She discovered, with delight, that she was pregnant. How wonderful to be having James's child, she thought. This child will certainly solidify our relationship and bring about our marriage at long last. When he finds that he is to be a father, he will surely want to hold the family close together, and marriage will secure a strong bond between James and me. James, although pleased about the baby, had found no time for a wedding before his unexpected incarceration.

During his months of imprisonment in Edinburgh Prison, Anna remained in the cottage on the Bothwell estate. She occupied her days mainly with gardening, reading and writing letters. She frequently sought information about James through acquaintances in Edinburgh and elsewhere. She learned very little, either because the persons contacted did not know anything about him or were reluctant to say anything about a controversial character for fear it might cause them trouble.

As the birth of her child approached, she could think of little else, even of James. She spent a great deal of time sewing and knitting clothes for the baby.

The servants in the castle had always been very kind to Anna. When they learned of her pregnancy, they admonished her, "You must be careful of your diet and get plenty of exercise." They watched over her with kindness, brought fine meals to the cottage and supplied other needs as her time of delivery approached.

"When your time comes," they insisted, "you must come to the castle where we have prepared a room for you and where we can assist with the birth."

"You are most kind. Thank you," Anna said. One day in June 1562, Anna knew the time had come and went to see the servants who showed her to the room. The baby arrived after only about three hours.

"My, what a fine boy you have, madam," one of the servants said as she showed Anna her son. Although she still felt weak, Anna eagerly reached for her baby who, she immediately realized, looked just like James.

"He's beautiful! And I'm sure he'll grow as strong as his father."

"What will you name him?" the woman asked.

"I shall call him William, after a favorite cousin. I hope James will approve that name."

After two weeks in the castle, Anna yearned for the comfort and familiarity of the cottage so she and her son moved back there. Soon life settled into a routine, and she watched William grow steadily. Months went by, however, and still there was no word about James.

The lonesome period of his long absence would have been intolerable for Anna were it not for William. Caring for William over these months kept her busy and relatively content. In the absence of James, Anna would often talk to her son even though he was unable to understand what she said.

Although Anna's love for James remained strong and she thought about him every day, at the same time she grew weary of waiting for his return. She could not keep from wondering if he would ever return to her or if he really loved her. She heard the news of his escape from prison in Edinburgh castle, his capture in England and his long incarceration in a prison in northern England.

She often felt discouraged since there was no indication as to when he could return to Scotland.

"William," she told him one day in August, "I heard today that your father managed an incredible escape from Edinburgh prison. Unfortunately, he is not able to come home to us yet. I do not know where he is now."

Anna decided in April 1563, that there was so much uncertainty about James's return, that she would leave Scotland and take her son William for a visit with her parents. She obtained passage on a ship that took her and the boy to Copenhagen, Denmark. She remained with her parents for an extended stay. Perhaps she could learn something here about her dear James although that seemed a remote possibility.

Anna was warmly welcomed home by her parents, but she was not entirely comfortable entering the home she had left so abruptly a few years earlier. She recalled the admonishments of her parents as she had excitedly told them of her intention to go to Amsterdam with her lover and marry him.

"We are delighted to have you back home, Anna, and to have little William with us. What a fine looking boy." Anna's mother was warm and welcoming. She kissed and hugged them both.

"I, too, am very pleased to see you, Anna," her father said as he kissed her. Then he leaned over to look more closely at William who nestled shyly in his mother's arms.

"We'll have some good times together," the grandfather said to William.

Anna's parents obviously wanted to make her feel comfortable at home and would have been happy to have her stay permanently. They were quite sensitive to her feelings, however, and did not bring up to her their earlier admonishments. Yet she recalled quite vividly her father's suggestion that she and James have the wedding performed in Copenhagen and then go to Amsterdam or Scotland. Perhaps in retrospect they were right but she had no wish to discuss the matter with her father. She thought it was difficult enough to realize that she had failed in three years to win the husband she sought. She did not need to be told that she had made a serious mistake in the early stage of her relationship with James.

Her father was surprisingly circumspect about the situation in which Anna found herself. He showed great affection toward her and William and made every effort to have a positive influence on Anna's readjustment to life in the family home. Her mother too showed a sympathetic understanding for her difficult circumstances and that was greatly appreciated by Anna. Nevertheless, Anna remained sad at times when she thought about the uncertainty of James situation. She longed for favorable news about him.

After their first day at home, Anna spoke to her father about James.

"Do you think, Father, that in your position as naval advisor to King Frederick, you might be able to obtain information about James through diplomatic channels?"

"Why yes, I can certainly try. I will talk with the Foreign Minister. I have a good relationship with him, and I am sure he would be willing to have his staff make inquiries at the British Foreign Office in London."

"Thank you Father. That would be wonderful," Anna responded. "I would like to know where he is now located and whether he is good health. Are there are still charges pending against him? If he is in prison, when might he be released? And anything else they can learn."

"I will do what I can, dear," Trondson replied.

Here in the Danish capital she might actually have a better opportunity to obtain information about James than in Edinburgh.

CHAPTER 7

Anna, Her Son And Dortea in Scotland Together

"Father," Anna said to Trondson after several weeks visiting in her parents' home, "could you again inquire through diplomatic channels about the status of my James. I must soon decide what to do with my life and that information is crucial."

"Yes, of course, dear," he replied. "I'll do so tomorrow." So far he had received no information about the Scottish admiral.

She felt increasing urgency about obtaining information about James.

Admiral Trondson had no difficulty making inquiries through the Ministry of Foreign Affairs. Trondson's past inquiries through diplomatic channels had been unproductive. Finally, in June 1563, her father had some news to report.

"I have just been informed by the Ministry of Foreign Affairs that the Earl of Bothwell met with Queen Elizabeth recently and, after their discussion of his case, she told him he was free to leave England."

"Oh, what wonderful news!" she exclaimed. "I must go back to Scotland right away!"

Trondson wondered whether this news was really so good for Anna. He certainly no longer had a high opinion of Bothwell. Trondson had no doubt that the man would continue to avoid making a commitment to Anna and would instead keep on misleading her into thinking they would some day marry. Now, for the first time since Anna had returned to Denmark, her father felt he should speak frankly to her.

"I am inclined to say to you, my dear, that the Earl of Bothwell may never become your husband. He is an elusive man whose political ambitions outweigh all else. Look how long you have waited for him to decide on marriage. Three years!"

"I know only too well how long the wait has been!" Anna exclaimed. "But I still love him so much I cannot give him up. And now that we have a child I am sure he will come back to me. I will continue to search for him, and someday I will marry this man somewhere, wherever I find him."

Trondson sighed.

"All right, dear."

He had tried to be understanding and patient with her. But he realized it would be fruitless to plead with her to reconsider the wisdom of her choice. He decided there was nothing he could do to persuade his daughter to give up her feelings for the man who had promised her marriage but so often found reason to postpone the event.

"I must return to Scotland as soon as possible now. I want to see James as soon as I can."

Trondson pondered her intention for a time and then said, "You do not know that he has, in fact, returned to Scotland. Why not wait here until you know for certain where he is located?"

She expected such a logical response from him and simply stated her conviction. "He is a Scotsman and loves his country. I feel sure he will return to his homeland at the first opportunity. I want to be there when he arrives in Scotland, if he has not already returned."

Then a fresh thought came to him.

"Why don't you take your sister Dortea with you. She will be good company and needs a chance to meet some new people."

"That's a wonderful idea," Anna said. "I will ask her to go with me. I do hope she will be agreeable to the trip."

"Both of you could return to Denmark whenever you wish," Trondson said, hoping to make it clear that he was skeptical of Anna's permanent residence in Scotland.

Anna had a long conversation with Dortea and, at first, the older sister was reluctant to leave Copenhagen where she had many friends and enjoyed the social life. She had no strong attachment to any Danish man, however, and on reflection thought the proposed trip to Scotland might be a good break from the Copenhagen social life.

Dortea was very fond of her sister. They would be good traveling companions she thought. Dortea knew very well the great love Anna felt for Bothwell and the many disappointments her sister had experienced in that relationship. Perhaps, Dortea felt, she could make Anna's return to Scotland easier, particularly if her lover failed to appear.

Dortea, two years older than Anna, was somewhat shy and quiet. Where Anna was quick to smile in conversations with almost anyone, Dortea was more reserved and serious in demeanor. In contrast to Anna's brunette hair, Dortea was very blond. Only five feet tall, Dortea was not as thin as her sister, but to say that she was plump would be an exaggeration.

"Let's make arrangements for travel to Scotland immediately," Anna suggested.

"Oh, yes," Dortea agreed. "We can go to the port in the morning and try to find a ship that will depart soon."

Anna and Dortea made arrangements the following day for the long voyage to Edinburgh. Fortunately, they found a merchant ship with some passenger accommodations that was scheduled to depart Copenhagen for Edinburgh within a week. During the next few days, they enthusiastically packed their belongings for the trip, which would be Dortea's first journey to Scotland.

In five days, they departed on a merchant ship carrying Danish products to Scotland. The two sisters enjoyed each other's company en route and the young William proved to be a good sailor, popular with the few other passengers and the ship's crew.

"I'm glad the weather has been so pleasant during the voyage," Anna commented after the first day at sea. "Usually, crossing the North Sea is pretty rough. We are lucky."

"Perhaps it is a good omen for our stay in Scotland. Maybe it means you will soon see your James," Dortea suggested.

"I hope you are right." Anna replied and became pensive.

As they proceeded down the Firth of Forth, Anna was able to point out familiar sights to Dortea. "There on the left is Seton Castle, one of the finest in Scotland."

"It is very impressive," Dortea said.

On arrival at the port of Leith, the two sisters needed a carriage to take them to the Bothwell estate. Several carriages were in the harbor area in search of customers. While Dortea and William stayed with their baggage, Anna approached one of the drivers.

"Please take us to Crichton Castle," Anna requested. "Do you know the way?"

"Yes, of course," he replied.

They went directly to the Castle rather than to the nearby cottage that was her temporary home. Anna was anxious to learn news of James. She expected he would be there to welcome her. When the two young women and William appeared at the doorway, they were warmly greeted by the servants.

"Is the Admiral at home?" Anna asked impatiently of the head servant.

"No Madam. We have not seen him in more than a year," the servant replied. Anna could not hide her disappointment.

"But I was told that Queen Elizabeth let him go free!" she said.

"That is true," the servant replied, "but instead of coming to Scotland, he then went to Paris, and as far as we know he is still there. We do not know when he will return to his home."

Anna was exasperated. Why, she asked herself, had she not taken her father's advice and inquired further as to where James had actually gone after he left England? Why had she simply assumed that he would return to Scotland?

Anna, William and Dortea went to the cottage on the estate and they settled into the small house together.

As Anna rested, she considered how she might learn of James's location in Paris so she could write to him there. More to the point, she could then ascertain when he might return to Scotland.

"I think Queen Mary's attitude toward James is probably the key to James's return," Anna said to Dortea.

"Do you think she would help you contact him?" Dortea asked.

"I hope so. One of the first things I want to do in Edinburgh is to arrange an audience with Queen Mary and find out exactly where James stands with the queen."

"You have told me that it might be risky for James to return to Scotland since he escaped from the Edinburgh prison. Wouldn't the queen place him in prison again if he returned to Scotland?"

"I don't know, but it has been almost a year since he escaped from Edinburgh prison and much has changed since then. When I heard that Queen Elizabeth had released him from the English prison, I hoped Queen Mary would be ready to let him come back. After all, he spent a long time in English prisons. The Scots, who hate the English, probably resent the way a Scotsman was treated in England. Therefore, I would expect much sympathy for Bothwell in Scotland now."

"But it was Queen Mary who ordered Bothwell's imprisonment here and she may still feel the same way about him."

"That is why I must talk with the queen. The fact that Queen Elizabeth released him from the Tower of London may have caused Queen Mary to have a more generous attitude toward him now. Don't forget, too, that James performed a great service for Mary Queen of Scots when he escorted her ships from France to Scotland. She will not have forgotten that assistance despite the incident that led to James's imprisonment."

Anna prepared a message for Queen Mary:

> "Your Highness Queen Mary:
>
> I recently arrived in Scotland with the intention of seeing the Lord Admiral James Hepburn, Earl of Bothwell. Unfortunately, I find that he is now in France. I would be most grateful if you would meet with me in the near future as I am anxious to know his present status as a Scotsman and when he may be expected to return to Scotland.
>
> Respectfully,
> Miss Anna Trondson"

She arranged with one of the Chrichton servants to deliver the message to the queen in Holyroodhouse Palace.

In a few days she received the following reply from the queen's secretary:

>"Miss Anna Trondson:
>   "In response to your request, Queen Mary would be willing to meet with you on Monday, July 20, 1563 at ten o'clock in the morning in Holyroodhouse palace.
>
>David Riccio, Secretary"

At the appointed time, Anna appeared at Holyroodhouse with the queen's message in hand to show the palace guard. She brought her sister Dortea with her, leaving William with a servant. Soon the two women were ushered into the palace and led to a drawing room where a man was seated at a desk.

"Good morning!" he said to Anna and Dortea as he rose from his chair. "What a pleasure to see you again, Miss Anna Trondson. And I am also pleased to meet your sister Dortea." She bowed to him.

"I am delighted to see you again also, Lord John," Anna said.

"As Anna knows, I am Lord John Stewart, brother of the queen. She will be here in a short while. In the meantime, she asked me to greet you and tell you that she will be a little late for your meeting." Lord John was the more amiable of the half brothers of Queen Mary. He had a good relationship with James Hepburn and had often tried to smooth relations between his brother, Lord James, and the Earl of Bothwell.

"While waiting, let me tell you a little about the palace," Lord John suggested.

"That would be most interesting," Dortea replied.

""Having lived here many years, I am quite familiar with its history," he began. Then he proceeded to tell about the early development of the palace and various works of art and several artifacts of interest.

"What an interesting palace," Dortea exclaimed.

"Tell me about your voyage from Denmark to Scotland," he asked.

"We were fortunate that the weather was relatively good en route," Dortea answered, "and Anna pointed out castles and other sights as we proceeded through the Firth of Forth to Leith," she continued.

"I trust your sister, the queen, is now well adjusted to Scotland," Anna interjected. "It must have taken considerable time to relearn the ways of the Scotch after many years in Paris."

Anna was on the verge of asking about his wife, Lady Janet, but then recalled that Lord John had divorced Bothwell's sister as the marriage had not been agreeable.

After a time, the queen entered.

Lord John spoke first, "Mary, let me introduce Anna Trondson and her sister Dortea."

"We are pleased to meet your highness," Anna spoke for both of them. Dortea smiled and bowed as did Anna. With the introductions completed, Lord John excused himself. As he left, he said to Anna and Dortea, but with his eyes focused on Dortea, "I hope I shall have the pleasure of seeing you again very soon."

"I would like that," Dortea replied with obvious interest.

Queen Mary got right to the point of the meeting, addressing Anna, "You expressed a desire to know the status of the Earl of Bothwell. I shall be quite candid in saying that he caused me considerable grief two years ago when he threatened my abduction."

"The admiral spent a great deal of time in prison both in Scotland and in England as a result of his alleged bad behavior," Anna replied, emphasizing the word alleged. "Are you willing now to permit him to return to his homeland?"

"Given the uncertainty of his guilt and the time he served in prison, I would have no objection to his return."

"I am pleased to hear you say that." Anna was clearly relieved. "Do you have any suggestion," Anna inquired further, "as to how I might reach him in Paris?"

"I do not know where he lives in Paris. Perhaps he is living with friends."

Queen Mary rose from her chair, signaling the end of the meeting.

"Thank you very much, your highness," Anna replied, "You have been most helpful." Then a servant ushered the two women to the exit.

As they departed the palace in a carriage, Anna said to her sister, "I am so glad we talked with the queen. Now I know James can return. Unfortunately, he does not know that and I do not know how to inform him of that fact."

"If he really wants to return, and he probably does," Dortea suggested, "he will make inquiries in Paris and learn that he can do so far as the queen is concerned."

"I suppose you are right," Anna said, "but how long will it be before he is back in Scotland? I guess I must be patient a while longer."

"When he does return," Dortea added, "you will want to be here."

"Yes, definitely."

Anna convinced herself that James's ties to Scotland were too strong for him to remain in France for long. Surely he would return soon.

She and Dortea enjoyed living together in the cottage on Bothwell's estate. They found much to discuss and many things to do in the Edinburgh area.

"I am so glad you came along with me and William to Scotland," she said to her sister more than once. "You are such great company for me in the absence of James."

"It has been very pleasant for me as well," Dortea said. "I am happy here."

One day not long after the palace visit, a note for the two of them arrived from Lord John. He invited Anna and Dortea to a party on his estate near Edinburgh. They were delighted to accept.

"There seems little doubt that Lord John is particularly interested in you," Anna said to her sister. "It was apparent during our meeting in the palace that he was attracted to you."

"Well, I found him very congenial. I am looking forward to seeing him again and attending his party."

The small social gathering at the home of Lord John was enjoyed by both the Trondson sisters. Several close friends of the nobleman were present and they all indulged in wine, dinner and convivial conversation. During the evening, John and Dortea slipped out of the main salon for a time and talked privately.

"Would you like to go riding with me tomorrow on some trails on my estate?"

"That would be enjoyable," she replied warmly.

"I shall send a carriage to pick you up at nine in the morning. You will find the ride invigorating."

Anna realized that this invitation and others that followed frequently meant that Dortea and John greatly enjoyed each other's company.

"How serious is this relationship between the two of you?" Anna asked Dortea one day.

"We are very close, Anna. I love him very much and I know he loves me."

Anna asked the obvious next question. "Does that mean that you expect him to propose marriage?"

"I do expect he will. I hope so!"

"Does it concern you that his marriage to Lady Janet Hepburn did not last long?" Anna asked.

"No. He has told me all about her and I am convinced that she was at fault in ending that marriage. I am certain that he would be a steadfast husband."

As Dortea expected, Lord John did propose marriage to her and a large wedding was planned at his estate. The wedding was to be held in August 1563.

"I never dreamed when we left Denmark together," Dortea said to Anna, "that I would fall in love with a man in Scotland!"

"One never knows where love will be found," Anna said. "I am very happy for you. He seems like a perfect husband for you."

"What a wonderful day," Dortea said to Anna as they stood in a vestibule of the church waiting for the wedding to begin. "Do I look all right?" Church bells were ringing loudly in the belfry of the Protestant church. All was ready except that they had to wait for the arrival of Reverend John Knox.

"You look like the ideal bride Dortea," Anna replied.

"I only wish our parents could be here for this great day but everything happened so quickly there was not time for them to make the long journey to Scotland."

Reverend Knox walked from his office to the sanctuary and took his place at the chancel step. The organ played a hymn as Dortea walked down the aisle with her attendants, including Anna and William. John stood waiting for their arrival at the chancel. After the marriage ritual, Reverend Knox said in a booming voice, "I pronounce you man and wife." The bride and groom kissed and soon hurried down the aisle toward the door while guests and attendants cried out their congratulations, "May you live happily together."

Shortly, a sumptuous banquet was served after which the guests danced long into the night. The queen was present, of course, as was her politically powerful half brother, Lord James of Moray.

Anna participated in the marriage ceremony with mixed feelings. She was naturally very happy for her sister. At the same time, she could not help feeling sad that she had not experienced the same good fortune as her sister. She had waited so long for her marriage to James to be realized. How much longer must she wait for him? Since he remained in France she could only speculate about his present thinking. How she wished he would return!

One day in October 1563, while he and Dortea were riding, John's horse stumbled during a fast run along a mountain side on his estate. Dortea was riding a slower horse a short distance behind. She saw his horse fall, throwing the rider forward onto the ground. Dortea rushed to John and found him unconscious. Quickly, she rode to their home and obtained the help of servants who brought him back and placed him in bed. He never regained consciousness.

Dortea was heart-broken over her husband's untimely death. She turned to her sister, Anna, for consolation.

"We had such a wonderful few months together," she cried. "I can't believe he is gone. What am I to do?"

"It was a terrible tragedy," Anna sympathized, "I know how happy you were together. Come and stay with William and me again."

"Thank you, Anna. I would like that," Dortea replied.

During the next several days, Anna and Dortea talked of their misfortunes, Dortea losing a fine husband after only a few months of happy marriage and Anna, not only separated from her fiance for an extended period but unsure of his intentions when he did return.

"Have you decided what you shall do now, Dortea?" Anna asked one day.

"I must return to Copenhagen, see our parents and try to rebuild my life," she said. "I can no longer be happy in Scotland. Will you come with me? Perhaps, there we can both start anew."

"No, Dortea, I cannot do that. I must wait for James's return. Until he comes, I'll be well occupied raising William."

The following week, Anna said a tearful goodbye to Dortea at the port of Leith. Her sister kissed William and then boarded a ship that soon was on its way to Copenhagen.

"Oh dear, how I will miss my sister," she said to William as they climbed into the carriage that carried them back to the cottage. Although too young to understand Anna's concern, William was nevertheless a great comfort to her.

When she was alone, she reflected on Dortea's suggestion that she return to Copenhagen with her. "I sometimes wonder," Anna said to herself, "why I do continue to stay here waiting for James to return. Since he has not communicated with me, maybe he really does not care about me. But he must know about our child's birth. Surely he feels a love for his small family and want to see his son. I must continue to be patient. I hope he is not in some sort of difficult circumstances in Paris."

Little did Anna realize how much longer she would have to wait for James to return. The rest of 1563 passed and he did not come home. Then all of 1564 also passed while he remained in France. Not until the summer of 1565 was there an indication that he might soon return to Scotland. William was now more than three years old.

During this long period of James's absence, Anna left Scotland for short periods. The first occasion was in June 1564 when she went to Norway to attend the wedding of her sister, Maren, in

Stavanger. Before she left, Lady Sinclair, mother of James Hepburn, who was very fond of William, pleaded with Anna to leave the two year old in her care, and Anna reluctantly agreed. Lady Sinclair was a wealthy widow and able to do everything for the boy. It was very evident to Anna that his grandmother loved William dearly.

"Don't worry about your child while you are away," she said, "he will be in very good care. I shall greatly enjoy having him with me during the weeks of your absence. Stay as long as you like with your sister in Norway."

"I shall miss my little boy so much," Anna replied. "William is such a lovable and inquisitive child."

Anna sailed from Leith on a Norwegian ship. Lady Sinclair and William were on the pier waving goodbye. A few days later, she was met in Stavanger by Maren and several other relatives and friends.

"Oh Anna, how great it is to see you after so many years." They embraced and then others greeted Anna warmly. Anna and Maren had not been together since before Anna met James in the summer of 1560.

"Where is William?" Maren asked.

"He is in the care of Lady Sinclair, his grandmother, while I am in Norway."

"I would have liked to see him, but his grandmother no doubt will enjoy caring for him."

"When he is a little older, I'll bring him with me on another trip to my homeland."

"This time, you can be of much help to me in the preparations for my wedding," Maren said to Anna as they rode in the carriage to her home in Stavanger.

"I'll be happy to do all I can. Tell me about your husband to be."

"You recall from my letter that his name is Olav Jonsson Thieste," Maren said. "He is the owner of a large estate located not far from this city. In fact, we'll be able to continue living in his fine home in the city while he manages the nearby farm. He has many people working for him."

"He must be quite successful," Anna commented.

"Yes but that is far less significant than the fact that I love him very much."

"You are so right. Nothing is more important," Anna responded.

Maren then shifted the conversation. "Tell me about your life in Scotland. The last I knew, James was in France. Has he returned to Scotland yet?"

"I am sorry to tell you that he remains in France. I continue to live on his estate with William, waiting for his return. It seems my life is largely one of waiting for him. In the meantime, I am raising my son alone as best I can."

"And I guess James has never seen William," Maren added.

"That is right. James was in Edinburgh prison when William was born. He escaped, went to England where he was imprisoned again until Queen Elizabeth allowed him to go to France. I am hopeful that Queen Mary will allow him to return to Scotland soon."

"Is there a reasonable prospect that he will do so soon?"

"I believe the circumstances developing in Queen Mary's government make it quite likely that he will return to Scotland in the very near future," Anna said optimistically.

"For your sake, I am very pleased to hear that."

Anna stayed a month in Norway, attending Maren's elaborate wedding and then traveling to the Hardanger Fjord area and to Bergen to visit with various other relatives and friends. In late July, she sailed from Bergen to Scotland. After taking her things from the port to the cottage, she went to the home of Lady Sinclair to reclaim William.

"William, my dear boy, how glad I am to see you." She hugged and kissed him.

"Mama, look at my toys." He held out a carved wooden horse and wagon.

"He has been an absolute delight," Lady Sinclair said.

"I am so glad to know that. I was apprehensive that he would be a nuisance to you," Anna said.

"Oh, no! He's adorable. I will be extremely pleased whenever you can leave him with me."

They talked awhile about Anna's travel to Norway and the outlook for James's return to Scotland. Lady Sinclair shared Anna's optimism that he would soon be home again. Then it was time for mother and child to leave.

"Come, William, say goodbye to grandmother; we must go home."

The optimism about James return, shared by Anna and his mother, proved to be unwarranted. Continued passage of time without his appearance weighed heavily on Anna. As if that was not disappointment enough, she received more bad news in January 1565. A letter from her mother told her that her father was very ill and might not survive more than a few months. Anna decided to travel to Copenhagen in February and see him.

The storms of the North Sea were particularly severe in February but she nevertheless felt it important to visit her father as soon as possible. Otherwise, she might never see him again. A Scottish merchant ship was scheduled to sail from Leith port to Copenhagen and she arranged passage.

For the second time, she asked Lady Sinclair to look after her son during her absence. The grandmother was delighted to do so, and William was quite content to stay with his her once again. Anna left him with full confidence that he was in good hands.

After a very rough trip to Copenhagen, she arrived in her former home town.

"Anna, I am so glad you are here," her father said as she entered his bedroom where he lay extremely ill with a weak heart. "I was afraid I might never see you again."

"I could not bear staying away while you are so ill," she said, "mother wrote to me that you were quite sick."

"Where is your son, William? I would like to see him too."

"I thought it best for him to stay with his grandmother this time. Traveling by ship in winter is not easy, as you know well."

"How well I remember storms of the North Sea. I could tell you some good stories about those rough waters." Now he showed the strain of their conversation and she cautioned him to rest quietly.

"Mother, how bad is his condition," Anna asked later. "He seems to tire very easily. I have never seen him so weak."

"I am afraid your father is seriously ill, Anna, even though he has had the best of care. The doctor says he may live only a few weeks or perhaps months but there is little that can be done for him."

"I have no reason to hurry back to Scotland so I will stay a long while this time," Anna promised.

"That will be a great comfort to both your father and me."

Her mother inquired about her life in Scotland and asked when she expected James to return from France. Anna had to give the same answers she had given to many others who made similar inquiries, that it was very difficult to guess when he might return and that she had been so often disappointed when her expectations proved baseless. Her mother then asked about William; Anna spoke warmly about the boy. She assured her mother that Lady Sinclair loved the boy dearly and was taking good care of him while Anna visited Denmark.

Kristoffer Trondson gradually became weaker and weaker over the course of two weeks. One day, the doctor told the family that he doubted the old man could last through the following night. His prediction proved correct. In the morning, he breathed his last breath. Karen, Anna and a Lutheran minister were at his bedside. Both women cried softly. What a tremendous loss.

Arrangements were made for funeral services and an impressive service was held in a few days later with many mourners present including King Frederick and a large number of naval officers.

Anna remained with her mother another ten days to help her adjust to the new circumstances. "What will you do now, mother? Will you continue to live in this home in Copenhagen?"

"It is difficult to make a decision on such a matter right now, but I am inclined to return to Norway, the land of my birth. Since all of my other daughters are living there I think I would be more content in my home country than in Denmark. Even Dortea has recently moved to Norway after returning briefly to Denmark from Scotland."

"I think it probably would be wise for you to move to Norway, Mother," Anna replied. "If I ever find it necessary to move from Scotland, I, too, would move to Norway. When I was in Norway last summer, I found it tempting to stay there rather than continuing my almost endless wait for James in Scotland. But I cannot give up my love for James despite his long absence. I still believe that he will come back to me."

"I know how you feel, Anna. A woman cannot give up her true love voluntarily. Your father was a trial for me at times during our marriage but I could not consider giving him up until death itself took him."

After nearly a month in Copenhagen, Anna sailed again to Scotland, recovered her child from Lady Sinclair, took up life once again on the Crichton estate, and continued her wait for James. As she settled into a routine, she sought any news that might provide some basis for hope that James would soon return.

CHAPTER 8

James Returns to Scotland

In 1565, While Anna and her son remained in Scotland and James continued to live in Paris exile, a number of European nobles sought to interest the widow, Mary Queen of Scots, in marriage. She was one of the most eligible candidates for marriage among women of European royal families of that time. She was not only a queen but also a young, bright and beautiful woman. A devout Catholic, she was interested only in marrying someone of the same faith. Accordingly, efforts were made to promote a marriage between Mary and Don Carlos, son of King Philip II of Spain, an aggressive leader against the Reformation. But Scotland had become Protestant some years earlier, and John Knox thundered against a proposed marriage of Mary and Don Carlos.

"Absolutely not! We will not tolerate having the Catholic Don Carlos in Scotland." The idea of marriage to Don Carlos was dropped soon.

During the first half of 1565, another possible mate for Queen Mary was suggested, namely, Lord Henry Darnley of England. Very significantly, too, he was a Catholic although his adherence to that faith was weak.

Word reached Queen Mary that Darnley wished to visit Scotland. Darnley was a young and handsome nobleman with some royal blood of both England and Scotland. Queen Mary wrote to Queen Elizabeth requesting that she approve the visit and the request was granted. Darnley traveled to Edinburgh. He and Mary became well acquainted but, within a few weeks of his arrival, he became quite ill. During his illness, she looked after him at Stirling Castle. Before long, she fell completely in love with him.

A few months after they first met, Henry Darnley said, "My dear Mary, will you marry me? I know that some Scottish people with strong feelings against England will object. Also, some English people who hate Scotland will object to our coming together as husband and wife. But I think a marriage between us could, over the long run, bring about significantly better relations between our two countries. More importantly, I love you, Mary."

"I love you dearly, Henry, and I am happy to marry you. I, too, realize that feelings among the people of both Scotland and England have, at times, led to emotional outbursts against their neighbors. but I agree that it is unlikely there will be any lasting ill will between our two peoples as a result of our marriage. In any case, I love you and wish to marry you."

Queen Mary's cousin, Queen Elizabeth, when advised of Mary's intention to marry Darnley, became furious.

"I strongly object to this marriage," Queen Elizabeth stated. In her objection, she was not very consistent. Having already approved Darnley's visit to the court of Queen Mary, Elizabeth must have known the interests of both Mary and Henry. She probably had second thoughts about the wisdom of a Catholic marriage in Scotland.

Young Darnley's ambitious Catholic mother had vigorously promoted the marriage and Queen Elizabeth deeply resented this involvement of Henry's mother. As a result, his mother was sent to the Tower of London. Elizabeth then sent an envoy, Throckmorton, to Scotland to persuade Queen Mary to change her mind about the marriage. Mary, however, was adamant that she would marry Darnley.

The wedding was held on July 22, 1565. Prior to that event, Mary gave Darnley the coveted title of Duke of Albany. At the wedding, the two exchanged vows in the presence of guests after which Mary went to her private chapel alone to celebrate mass. Later, there were great festivities including a banquet, music and dancing. Thus within a remarkably short period of about six months, the two were united in marriage. The heralds proclaimed that Darnley should henceforth be named and styled "King of this, our Kingdom."

Queen Mary's meddlesome but politically influential brother, Lord James Moray, objected strongly to the marriage of the two Catholics and refused to attend the wedding. Moreover, he declined to attend an important meeting of nobles following the marriage. Worse, he spread rumors reflecting adversely on Mary and Darnley. He told a number of his Protestant colleagues that Mary was attempting to bring about the restoration of the Catholic faith as the principal religion of Scotland. As a leading Protestant political leader, Moray sought the strong support of Protestant nobles in opposing the new Catholic leadership of Scotland.

"How could you embarrass me in such a humiliating way," she complained to him in the castle soon after the wedding, "not only refusing to attend our wedding but also speaking critically of the marriage among many of your noble friends?"

"This is a Protestant country," he replied calmly, "I feel it is my duty to try keeping it so." He stormed out.

Queen Mary was furious over her brother's vocal opposition to her marriage. Accordingly, Lord Moray was "put to the horn," that is, outlawed for having refused to appear before his sister to apologize for his behavior. His properties were seized and he was accused of rebellion. Moray was pursued around Scotland by nobles loyal to the queen. This so-called "chase-about" in Scotland was followed by Moray's fleeing to England where he expected to receive support for his cause from Queen Elizabeth. He was bitterly disappointed when both Queen Elizabeth and the English Council denied him support.

Religion was a major factor defining the loyalties of various Scottish clans and nobles. The vast majority of the people of Scotland, as Protestants, resented the Catholic royalty but a significant number of them grudgingly tolerated these leaders. Even though the queen kept her practice of the Catholic faith strictly private, the people knew the queen's taste in religion and they often expressed their dislike of her religious preference.

Surprisingly, despite the predominance of Protestants in Scotland, there was sufficient support for Queen Mary and Henry Darnley to prevent any significant eruption against the couple. The Catholic Lord Lennox, father of the new king, was, of course, supportive of his son and Queen Mary. Lady Margaret, wife of Lord Lennox, came from the important Douglas clan in Scotland, a clan headed by the aggressive leader, Earl of Morton, and he too supported the queen and new king. In contrast, the Protestant Hamilton clan was perennially opposed to Queen Mary and was particularly active in opposition to her marriage. On balance there was far less loyal support for the heads of state than Mary wished.

"I recall so well the Earl of Bothwell's support for my mother when she was regent," she mused. "Unfortunately, there are few like him in Scotland. If I had not been so pressured by the deceptive Lord James to place him in prison, Bothwell would now be here, a loyal and useful supporter beside me. How I wish he were here now! Although a Protestant, he was always supportive of the Catholic royal family of Scotland."

"Scotland will never again become a Catholic nation," cried John Knox, the stormy Protestant pastor and outspoken reformer. "We will not rest until the royal family of this country accepts the Protestant faith of the majority of its people." He made no secret of his strong distaste for the queen's adherence to the Catholic faith. Quite the contrary, he vigorously opposed the Catholic royalty. On a number of occasions they met and he strongly urged Mary to convert to the Protestant faith. Some of these confrontations were loud and fiery. She never conceded points to Knox during these arguments and steadfastly held firm to her religious views. Unfortunately for the queen, Knox enjoyed substantial influence among the Scottish people and he was very influential in persuading the Scots to hold fast to their Protestant beliefs and continue their opposition to the queen's religion.

Since both royals were subjects of substantial and growing criticism in the country, Mary knew she needed to bring a strong supporter into her small circle of political supporters, someone of unquestioned loyalty, courage and strength, someone who would not hesitate to deal with the powerful forces arrayed against her. In her view, the Earl of Bothwell fit that need precisely. She recognized, of course, that he could be reckless at times, as in the case of the threatened abduction incident, but she felt that she could trust him. She therefore dictated a message to the Scottish ambassador in France requesting that he contact Bothwell and deliver to him a letter urging his return to Scotland as soon as possible.

The warm relationship between the queen and Darnley cooled significantly during the fall and winter following the July wedding. While Mary had a keen interest in governmental affairs and devoted much time to these activities, Darnley had little interest in the processes of government. The two lacked a common interest in their essential roles as royal leaders. In contrast to her serious interest in government, his interests were frivolous and irresponsible.

Notwithstanding his lack of concern with government, Darnley persisted in pressing Mary and others for a certain official recognition in the form of the "crown matrimonial." If Mary approved this right and Parliament were to grant it, Darnley's power would be equal to hers while she lived and, significantly, would continue after her death if Darnley survived her.

Mary refused to initiate any action along these lines, at least in part because she was conscientiously concerned that he lacked interest in government. Why should he have that added power if he had no inclination to exercise any responsibility carrying out appropriate governmental functions?

During the fall, Mary discovered that she was pregnant. She was, of course, happy that she would have an heir. The impending event did not, however, bring the couple closer together as might have been expected. Their relationship continued to be influenced by fundamental differences in interests.

While Mary tended to the affairs of state, Darnley entertained himself in various ways. He drank excessively and gambled frequently. During some evenings, he went to wild parties in the town and took up with other women. Mary and Darnley moved farther and farther apart.

In Paris, the Scottish embassy received the urgent

communication from Queen Mary in August 1565 requesting that the office deliver an important message to Bothwell. The embassy had little difficulty locating the Scotsman as he was well known around the city. Within hours, they found him and asked him to report to the embassy immediately. The invitation surprised him and he wondered what it meant.

He had heard, of course, about the marriage in July of Queen Mary and Lord Darnley. Bothwell knew very well the tumultuous political conflicts in Scotland along with sharp religious conflict, intense clan rivalries and the inclination of rivals to fight one another rather than try to settle differences by debate and compromise. He was well aware of the stresses in Scottish society, particularly with Catholic heads of state in a fiercely Protestant land.

The admiral appeared at the embassy the following morning.

"Good morning, Mr. Ambassador," Bothwell greeted his host. "I have come in response to your invitation."

"Thank you for coming, Admiral," the ambassador replied. "I have a confidential letter for you from Queen Mary." He handed the sealed letter to him. She informed me in a general way about the contents of the message. "Please read it and then we can discuss the matter."

Bothwell read:

"Lord Admiral James Hepburn, Earl of Bothwell

Dear Lord James:

I recall very well the unfortunate circumstances that led to your incarceration in Edinburgh prison and your subsequent imprisonment in the Tower in London. For some time now you have enjoyed freedom in my beloved France and I trust you have done well there. Nevertheless, as a son of Scotland I am sure you yearn to return to your native land.

You are intimately acquainted with the many rivalries among the clans of Scotland. In particular, you know well the opposition I face from the Hamilton clan and others. I need you here in Edinburgh to help me deal with the forces opposing me. You have the courage and strength to cope with my enemies. I trust you as a loyal supporter.

I urge you to come to Edinburgh as soon as possible. It would be wise for you to travel here secretly to avoid any incident that might be instigated by either the English or my Scottish enemies.

Her Majesty, Queen Mary, August 5, 1565"

The still-ambitious Bothwell was pleased to learn that the queen needed him. She obviously was willing to forget the problems that led to his imprisonment in Edinburgh Castle. Here was an opportunity not only to return to his native Scotland but also to serve Queen Mary in a significant way. He was delighted!

"I am aware," the ambassador said to Bothwell, "that Queen Mary wants you to return to Scotland as soon as possible and assist her government. I am prepared to assist you financially in making the journey and will provide whatever assistance you desire with travel arrangements."

"That is very kind of you," Bothwell replied. "I will accept the financial aid but prefer to make my own travel arrangements."

One could not be too careful about choosing a ship, he thought, since someone in the embassy could be a conspirator against him. He knew very well that his enemies would like to intercept him en route to Scotland and see that he never arrived at his destination.

The following day, Bothwell dressed in a manner that would make him as inconspicuous as possible in public. He must be careful that no one identify and follow him. Leaving his room, he walked a short way to a place where he arranged for a carriage to take him to the port of Calais on the English channel.

Soon the carriage was on its way to the port. When he arrived there, he would find a fishing vessel that could take him to Scotland. The ship would have to be capable of making the voyage through the rough weather that often develops in the North Sea.

En route to Calais, Bothwell had time to consider how he would proceed. When the carriage reached the vicinity of the port, making its way through the congestion of stevedores, fishermen, nets, boxes, kegs and other obstacles, he had the driver head toward a cluster of fishing vessels. They stopped again. Bothwell paid the driver and stepped out of the carriage onto the pier. He studied the situation carefully as he strolled about the busy fishing dock. His eye caught a relatively large fishing vessel, and he walked over to a man loading a net onto the ship.

"Hello mate," Bothwell addressed him, "Can you show me to the captain of this vessel?" The sailor looked him over and continued his work.

"We have a full crew already and will cast off within a few hours," he said.

"I am not looking to join your crew. I have other business to discuss with the captain."

"In that case, you will find him in the wheel-house." The sailor pointed the way.

Bothwell boarded the ship and proceeded in the direction the sailor had indicated toward the bow of the ship in search of the captain.

He confronted an old salt who was making repairs on the steering wheel. "Are you the captain?" The man's hair and generous beard were gray, and he was dressed like his crewman in rough clothing. There was nothing pretentious about him.

"Yes, I am the captain—Captain Boule. If you want to join our crew it is too late. We have all the men we need."

"I am not looking for a job," Bothwell replied. "I am looking for passage to a rather distant port, and I wonder if you can take me there."

"Well, that would depend on the price you would be willing to pay. If it is more than I can earn fishing, then I might be willing to take you. Where do you want to go?"

"Scotland. You would drop me there and return to Calais without me."

"That is a long voyage. What would you pay me for the trip?"

"I will pay you fifty francs."

"Not enough for such a service. I need seventy francs."

"Sixty francs and no more," Bothwell said firmly, as if it was his final offer, "I will give you half now and the other half when we reach my destination."

"All right. I accept." Captain Boule took the thirty francs offered.

With that matter settled, the captain and Mr. McTavish, as Bothwell identified himself to the captain, were in full agreement on the voyage to Scotland. While Boule was a fisherman and not a transport operator, the captain reasoned that there would be ample opportunity for fishing during the return voyage. It should be a profitable run.

"Is your ship fully loaded with the supplies you need?" Bothwell asked.

"Yes, we are ready to sail," he replied.

"And we are agreed that we will depart quietly after dark?"

"Yes, but I would rather leave sooner."

"Well, I have my reasons," Bothwell said without revealing them. He was still wary that his enemies might learn of his planned arrival in Scotland and interfere with the voyage in some way. One could not be too careful.

That evening, the ship raised its sails and proceeded quietly and little noticed out of Calais.

At first, the weather was good with a strong, favorable wind from the southeast. As they proceeded northward beyond the English Channel, however, then encountered severe storms. The crew was kept busy adjusting the sails and protecting the nets and other gear from being washed overboard in the high seas. Admiral Bothwell was quite familiar with these waters and was not at all surprised by the challenging circumstances the captain faced in the North Sea. James recalled with a shiver his escape from the shipwreck in these waters about three years earlier.

After two days sailing along the English coast, Bothwell considered possible ports in Scotland where he might disembark. The port he definitely wanted to avoid was Leith near Edinburgh

since that one was the most risky in terms of possible confrontation
with his enemies. There were a few small ports south of Edinburgh
in the borders area which Bothwell knew intimately. Here his arrival
would be little noticed and he could travel inland to his Crichton
Castle with minimal danger.

"We are passing Newcastle now, Mr. McTavish, and we will
soon reach the Scottish coast. Have you decided yet where you
would like to disembark?" Captain Boule was anxious to drop his
passenger as soon as possible so he could return to fishing in waters
near France.

"There is a small Scottish port called Eyemouth located north
of Holy Island. It is located only a short distance inside the Scottish/
English border. This would be a good place for me to go ashore."

The captain was pleased that he did not have to go to the busy
port of Leith, near Edinburgh, which would have required a much
longer journey.

"That will be fine." Captain Boule replied. "We should reach
your port on the day after tomorrow, if winds are in our favor."

The next day, they passed Holy Island. They could see the
famous Lindesfarne Priory clearly. During the night, they passed
the last English port of Berwick-Upon-Tweed. Bothwell was on
deck early the following morning studying the coast carefully.

"We have now passed the border," Bothwell said. "The port of
Eyemouth should soon be visible. I suggest, Captain, that you sail
closer to shore. I can assure you that the water depths within a
hundred yards of the coast are safe. I know these waters well."

The captain followed his suggestion, but was nevertheless
cautious. Soon a small town came into view. As the ship moved
closer, they could see a pier and a few fishing boats in the quiet
port.

"I doubt that the water at the pier is deep enough for your
ship. One of your crew can lighter me to the pier."

They pulled down sails and dropped anchor as Bothwell
prepared to depart. He paid the captain the balance of the agreed
fare.

"You made a good voyage, Captain Boule, and I wish you well
on your return trip to Calais."

"Your boat is ready to take you ashore, Mr. McTavish. Good luck."

Bothwell climbed out of the boat onto the pier and walked toward the village. He could recall no acquaintance in this village and thought that no one would recognize him. That was exactly the way he wanted it.

His principal need now was a horse to ride through the borders area. On the edge of town he found a farmer who had a few horses.

"Good morning!" Bothwell addressed the farmer. "I just arrived in Eyemouth and am in need of a horse. Could you sell me one of your horses?"

"No, I need these horses on my farm."

"But I am willing to pay you a good price." Bothwell persisted.

"I could not run my farm without them. Try someone else."

Bothwell pressed him further, offering a price that surprised the farmer and caused him to change his mind. With the generous money received, the farmer reasoned, he could easily buy two horses from his neighbors.

Bothwell bought not only the horse but also a suitable saddle from the farmer. Then he started his long journey to Crichton Castle. He proceeded over the familiar Southern Uplands, following trails he had traveled many times over the years since he was a boy. It felt good to be in his home territory again.

All day Bothwell rode along the trails. With nightfall, he found a place along the trail where he tied his horse to a tree and prepared to spend the night. Since it was summertime, the night temperature was tolerable though cool in the hills. He wrapped himself in a blanket and obtained several hours of sleep. Early in the morning he ate some bread he had brought with him and also found some berries nearby. Then he climbed on his horse and continued his ride.

At mid-day, Bothwell arrived at Crichton Castle. His servants greeted him warmly, took his horse to a stable and brought food and drink to his room. He had a long rest. How wonderful it was to be home again!

His servants informed him that Anna had returned from Copenhagen two months earlier and had again settled into the cottage on the estate. Bothwell was somewhat surprised that Anna was still waiting for him. He hoped she did not still expect him to marry her; he had more ambitious goals. However, he decided that he might as well take advantage of her presence. That evening he walked over to the cottage and greeted her.

"Hello, my darling!" Bothwell surprised her as she opened the cottage door. He enveloped her with a big hug and kiss.

"What—What a surprise to see you." Anna could hardly believe her eyes! "When did you arrive, James? Where have you been?"

"I arrived from France today."

"I am relieved to see safely back in Scotland," she said coolly, "but I don't mind telling you that I have been quite bitter that you never took the trouble to write to me during these years you have been away. Why didn't you write and tell me something, anything? Do you really care about me?"

"Of course I still care for you," he lied. "Whatever the past, Anna, here I am and we are together again." Bothwell said more exuberantly, and kissed her again.

Just then, William came into the room. The father looked at the boy in surprise and said, "What a fine looking boy! Could you be my son?"

He lifted up the three year old and studied his features. Then he said, "Yes, I think you are my son."

Anna was disturbed by his questioning whether William was in fact their son but kept her thoughts to herself. She did not ask him whether he knew he had a son, assuming his mother or someone must surely have told him. It still troubled her that he had failed to communicate with her during his long absence from Scotland, but she could also feel herself falling under his spell once again. His enthusiasm was always contagious. Anna and James spent the evening together, and he left her cottage quietly early in the morning.

The following day, Bothwell rode to Edinburgh and called on Queen Mary at Holyroodhouse. His arrival was announced to her by an aide.

"Show him in," she said expectantly. Bothwell was quickly escorted into her reception room.

"Welcome to the Palace, Admiral. I am delighted that you received my message and that you were able to travel to Edinburgh so soon."

"Your Highness, I came as quickly as I could. Your letter seemed to convey a sense of urgency."

"Yes, you are right. There are matters requiring urgent attention. As you know, my brother, Lord Moray, objected strongly to my marriage to Lord Darnley and has opposed me in various ways. Moreover, John Knox has continued to object to my adherence to the Catholic faith. These men are seeking to gain support from various lords of Scotland who have so far been loyal to me. However, leaders of the opposition have achieved some success. I need someone to help me defend my position."

"As your loyal supporter, I shall do all I can to defend the Queen of Scotland."

"I am most grateful for your loyalty and your willingness to assist in strengthening my Government. I promise that your support will be well rewarded."

Bothwell withdrew from his audience with Queen Mary full of hope that he would be richly rewarded in the near future.

During the next several weeks, Bothwell had a number of audiences with the queen and her agents. She consulted him concerning the best approach to use in dealing with her enemies or opponents, seeking his advice on every detail of strategy and tactics. She also sought his advice on broad policy issues facing her government.

As a consequence of his heavy involvement in the queen's problems in Edinburgh, Bothwell had little time to spend with Anna.

"Why don't you spend more time with me?" she pleaded one evening when she found him in his castle.

"I have been extremely busy assisting the queen and her officials," he explained. "She depends on me at this critical time."

"I miss you!" she replied. "I thought we would be together more often when you returned. I have been alone so long."

"I am sorry. But my service to the queen must come before all else. When the pressures of the queen's demands on me are eased we'll be together all the time," he soothed. She retreated to her cottage as he departed for another official meeting.

As Bothwell left, he breathed a sigh of relief. Can't she let me have some freedom? Must she nag? I'll see her when I am in the mood. Maybe I will feel like it this evening. In the meantime, she can take care of the boy and do whatever else she needs to do. If I play my cards right with the queen, there are some real rewards coming my way.

CHAPTER 9

James Weds Lady Jean

The pressures of government affairs on Bothwell were intense during the weeks and months toward the end of 1565. Nevertheless, he found time for a new diversion. He began seeing a widow, Lady Jean Gordon. Although physically not very attractive, she was the wealthy sister of the powerful Lord Huntley. Lady Jean's manner was that of cool detachment from people, and therefore she hardly seemed suitable for the flamboyant Bothwell. However, Bothwell found her money and position among the leading nobility particularly attractive, much more important than personality. Lord Huntley considered Bothwell a friend, and he considered the admiral a good choice for his sister. He strongly encouraged the relationship. She was willing to marry Bothwell even though she showed little sign that she actually cared.

In the late fall, an announcement was made in Edinburgh that the Earl of Bothwell and Lady Jean Gordon were to be married in February 1566. When Anna learned of the impending marriage between James and Lady Jean Gordon, she was incredulous and rushed to see him at the earliest possible moment for verification of the dreadful news.

"Is it true that you will marry Lady Jean Gordon? What does this mean? How can you!" she demanded of Bothwell tearfully.

"It means that Lady Jean and I will be married," he stated bluntly.

"But you have promised to marry me! You promised and promised, and I have been waiting all these years. You told me you loved me. How can you just desert me?"

Bothwell looked aside. "I once thought it was a good idea for us to marry but I have changed my mind."

"Why didn't you tell me of your change of mind? Why did you take advantage of me and lead me to believe that some day we would be married? You deceived me! And then you did not even have the courage to tell me. I had to hear the news from others."

"Look, we had many good times together. That is all past. Now my life is changing and I shall soon be married to Lady Jean. Why can't you just accept that?"

"You have deceived me for years. I should have known that you would not keep your promise. You took advantage of me with promises, promises of marriage."

"I have tried to let you know more than once that we might not be suited to one another. Now, I have found someone I really want to marry. You should recognize that fact and not make a scene. You should have realized much sooner that we would never marry!"

There was a period of cold silence. Then Bothwell said, "I think we should simply say goodbye!" With that said, he hurried away.

Anna burst into tears. She finally had to accept the fact that Bothwell refused to marry her—after precious years during which she believed that he loved her and that he would marry her sometime. Now at last, she realized that this was the end of the affair. What a fool she had been to let him take advantage of her all these years.

How like his father! She now recalled stories told to her by people in Edinburgh who knew the late Patrick Hepburn. He too was deceptive and undependable. During his chaotic life, Patrick, like James, served years in prison and had been exiled for a time. Anna could now see how much alike were James and his father. She regretted that she had not realized earlier that James would not let anything interfere with the pursuit of his ambitions for position and wealth. How could she have been so blind? Well-placed women were merely stepping stones toward his achievement of power and riches. Other women, not so well placed, were merely objects of his occasional pleasure. Anna was now finally aware that she was one of these unfortunate other women.

Crying softly and with her thoughts in turmoil, she slowly walked to the cottage where she had spent so many, many months stretching into years. As soon as she could obtain passage on a ship to Norway she would leave Scotland forever. But what about William? He was the son of James as well as her. How would he react if she took William with her to Norway? She soon found out.

A few days after her confrontation with James, Anna went to the castle in the early evening and told him of her plans to leave.

"William and I are leaving Saturday on a ship bound for Bergen, Norway. I want you to know that you will be able to see him there if you are interested. You have never shown much interest or affection for him but perhaps some day you will realize what a fine boy he is and perhaps want to see him."

"What do you mean? Don't you realize that he is my son?" he responded angrily." Just because I have not spent as much time with him as I would like, because of my duties for the queen, doesn't mean that I would give him up to live in Norway."

"I don't understand you," she replied worriedly, "surely you do not intend to prevent my taking him with me to Bergen. You know I have raised him with no help from you whatever."

"Under Scottish law, the father has the primary right to keep the child," he said confidently, "and I certainly intend to assert my rights."

Anna began to sob. "You wouldn't be so terribly cruel as to take him from me after all I have done in raising him. I love William with all my heart."

"I have given some thought to his care," he replied coolly. "My mother, Lady Sinclair, has already agreed to care for him. You left the boy with her for long periods of time in the past and they got along fine. Before you leave the country, you will turn him over to her, and he will be raised properly. Now I must go to the palace."

Anna was distraught but knew she was defeated. "How can I bear to leave William?" Although Lady Sinclair loved the boy and would care for him very well, Anna would find it near impossible to be without him in Norway. Who knows when she would see him again? James was so cruel, caring little for the boy, yet not letting her take him. Weeping, she walked slowly back to the cottage to pack her things for the trip to Norway. How foolish she had been to believe James ever loved her; he was totally selfish and mean-spirited. How could she have ever loved him?

CHAPTER 10

The Admiral Flees Scotland

Only a month after the elaborate wedding of The Earl of Bothwell and Lady Jean Gordon at Crichton Castle, a crisis arose in Holyroodhouse Palace. The atmosphere in the palace became tense, stemming partly from the fact that Lord Darnley had become embittered that he had not been given the Crown Matrimonial thus denying him the authority he so desperately wanted. The issue had been a persistent bone of contention between Henry and Mary for a long time. He had become obsessive about the issue.

"Can you give me one good reason why I should not receive the Crown Matrimonial?" he demanded angrily of the queen one evening.

"Yes, I can," she replied unemotionally. "You show very little interest in government, seldom attending Parliament and rarely reviewing petitions from subjects or proposals for improvements in policies and programs."

"I attend those boring sessions of Parliament often enough, and there are plenty of others to review subjects' petitions," he yelled defensively. "Furthermore, as long as you deny me the rights I deserve, why should I take an active role in government?"

"You must demonstrate some interest in the process of government before I grant the rights you crave," she answered firmly.

"You are mean and stubborn," he screamed and left the room in a fit of anger. He went to his favorite tavern in Edinburgh and got drunk. Another irritant for him was that Bothwell, whom he detested, had an important role in the government. What right had Bothwell to have more influence in government than the king?

"Here I am the King of Scotland," Darnley told himself, "and that aggressive fellow has more responsibility than I have. It is not fair. It is humiliating."

Yet another source of Darnley's dissatisfaction with his situation was that the queen often spent long periods of time playing cards with her secretary, Riccio. She is much too friendly with him, Darnley felt, and sooner or later he was going to do something about it. It was not right that she relied increasingly on her secretary's views on various subjects rather than ask him, the king, for an opinion on issues.

As he sat alone drinking, still another irritation added to his sense of frustration and anger. Queen Mary was pregnant, and Darnley strongly suspected that the father was Riccio, rather than himself. The birth of the royal heir was expected in June, only a few months away. Darnley groused that the event would be widely celebrated throughout the land. What satisfaction was there for him since Riccio was very likely father of the child?

"Hello, your highness," a nobleman appeared at Darnley's table in the tavern, "what news have you from the palace?"

"Nothing good, Ruthven," Darnley replied bitterly. "The queen is probably playing cards with her secretary at this very moment."

Ruthven was one of a considerable number of nobles in Edinburgh opposed to the queen on both religious and policy grounds. Some of these nobles also shared Darnley's dislike of the queen's talented and amiable secretary, Riccio. One of these frequent critics was the nobleman, Ruthven.

"I share your disgust with that Italian secretary," Ruthven whispered to the inebriated king. "He has far too much influence over the queen. I think we can find a way to separate the two of them."

"How would you do that?" Darnley drunkenly asked.

"I have some friends who feel as we do, and they will help us eliminate Riccio once and for all. I think we can arrange it one evening later this week, if you are willing to go along with us."

"Good," Darnley said and displayed a wide grin of approval. "Just tell me what I have to do."

Shortly after, on an evening in March 1566, when the queen was meeting with Riccio in the palace, the conspirators carried out their nefarious plot. Among the group was Darnley. The men brazenly entered the queen's private room.

"We are here to free your highness from a bad influence," Ruthven said to the queen. He had a dagger in his hand.

"How dare you enter my private chamber without permission?" The queen demanded. The intentions of the men quickly became clear to both Mary and Riccio, however.

"Please protect me, your highness," Riccio pleaded and moved beside her. The attackers brushed by her roughly and grabbed the secretary. Mary was unable to do anything to protect her unfortunate secretary. And there was no one else around who could help the queen and her secretary. Ruthven brutally stabbed the loyal and capable Riccio many times and left him to die. With numerous stab wounds, he died almost immediately.

"What have you done!" cried the horrified queen.

"The foreigner will no longer be able to distract your royal highness," Ruthven sneered as he and his collaborators rushed out of the palace.

At the time of the murder, Bothwell and his close friend Huntly were elsewhere within the palace. Some of the queen's supporters suspected that these two men might also have been involved in the conspiracy. Loyal military aides of the queen searched for Bothwell and Huntly but could not find them because the two men, learning of the murder, realized the danger of being accused of involvement and avoided capture by jumping out of a palace window, hurriedly leaving the area. Although Mary no doubt was troubled by the suspicion that Bothwell might have been implicated in the crime, the force of Bothwell's personality convinced her of his loyalty to her.

Queen Mary was greatly depressed by Riccio's death. She was especially bitter toward her husband for his involvement in the crime.

"I do not understand," she said to her husband, "how you could be involved in such a hideous murder."

"It was necessary to get him out of the way because, in the view of several of us, he was having an undue influence over you in the affairs of government," Darnley said unconvincingly.

"He was a competent secretary but all important decisions were made by myself alone. He did not undermine my authority in any way."

"You do not realize how much you depended on him," Darnley countered.

She hated Darnley for his involvement in the sordid affair but, after a time, realized that his loyalty toward the queen was absolutely vital to the security of her own position as royal head of Scotland. Therefore, she sought to hide her true negative feelings toward Darnley, outwardly treating him as before. Gradually, in this way, she won back the loyalty of her husband.

"You should be aware that you are in as much danger as I am if a large number of noblemen decide to turn against me," she cautioned him. "Therefore, you had better stand with me rather than appear to be opposed to me on fundamental policies."

"I realize that," he said, "and I will do what I can to defend the crown.

Notwithstanding this practical compromise in her own self interest, she still hated Darnley.

Mary was in constant fear, during the months that followed the murder of Riccio, that something might happen to the baby she was expecting. She had to keep her feelings to herself as she had no one with whom she could confide.

The baby boy was born on June 19, 1566. As expected, there were great celebrations throughout Scotland. The boy was named James and was taken to Stirling Castle where he was put in the custody of Lord Erskine, Earl of Mars, the traditional custodianship of royal children.

King Henry Darnley showed very little feeling for the child, probably continuing to harbor the suspicion that the late secretary Riccio was the child's father.

"I am not certain whether I am the father," he candidly stated to Mary after the birth of the boy.

"Your suspicions are completely unwarranted," she said, "There is no possibility of anyone else being the father."

"I am unconvinced," he replied.

Despite her assurances, Darnley became extremely sullen. He and Mary spent less and less time together.

Increasingly, Mary turned for support and advice to three nobles: Moray, Bothwell and Huntly. Among them, Bothwell seemed the most supportive.

"My half brother, Lord James Moray, should be my closest advisor," she said to Bothwell one day. "He is not only closely related to me but has had long experience in parliament and government generally. Yet I find that he is usually opposed to me, criticizing my polices and urging me to change direction. He is, at times, deceitful."

"I have dealt with Lord Moray many times over the years," Bothwell replied candidly, "and I share your view that he is often deceitful and undependable. I would urge you to be very careful in your dealings with him. In my opinion, his real objective is to succeed you somehow as head of state, and he wants to undermine your position."

"You have spoken to me with remarkable candor. I appreciate it."

"I thank your highness," he said. Then changing the subject, he stated, "The Borders area, where I live, is often plagued by troublemakers of one sort or another. So far as I know you have never visited that part of Scotland. May I suggest that a visit by your highness to the area would be enlightening."

"I think that is an excellent idea. I need to see the Borders first hand."

In the fall of 1566, she and a military contingent went to the Borders area to deal with a number of disputes. Bothwell accompanied her to a number of meetings regarding these disputes. She was impressed with his leadership qualities in settling cases arising in this troublesome area.

Soon after the queen's visit, Bothwell, as the Lieutenant of the Borders, led a force of three hundred horsemen into a district where an open feud between contesting parties was being fought with guns and swords over ownership of stray cattle. Seeking to quell the fighting, Bothwell was seriously wounded and carried to Hermitage Castle.

When the queen heard of Bothwell's wounding, she set out on horseback from Holyroodhouse, to the Hermitage Castle. On the way, she was thrown from her horse and taken to Jedburgh for recovery and rest. She became gravely ill while there. Shortly after that incident, Bothwell was well enough to be carried to Jedburgh to see the queen.

"Your highness, I am sorry you had such a hard fall from your horse," Bothwell began, "I hope you are soon well enough to travel back to the palace."

"Thank you. I should be able to ride tomorrow. And how are you? I see you too are in recovery, but from wounds received in battle."

"I am almost well. I have been wounded before in these skirmishes."

"You are a strong supporter of mine, Admiral."

"I am indeed. Now I must leave you, your highness," Bothwell said, "I trust I shall see you soon in Edinburgh."

Later that day, Darnley arrived at Jedburgh from Edinburgh to see the queen. He stayed only briefly and showed little sympathy for her condition. He quickly returned to the palace. Mary traveled to the palace the next day with her escort of soldiers.

Two noblemen one day requested a private meeting with the queen. She agreed to meet with them.

"What is it you wish to speak with me about?" she asked them.

"The subject is very delicate and we hardly know where to begin," one of them said.

"Perhaps I can present the issue," the other said. "We are well aware, as are many noblemen in Scotland, that your relations with the king are very strained. We are most sympathetic with your highness and want to suggest a solution to the problem."

"We think the solution," interjected the other, "is for you to divorce Darnley which would be the best way out of the difficulty, best for your highness and for Scotland."

"I appreciate your candor and your good will in making this suggestion to me," she replied. "Unfortunately, the course you recommend has a serious disadvantage. Such action would mean that the church would almost certainly declare my marriage to Darnley null and void and, as a consequence, my son James would be considered illegitimate. As a result, my son would not be in the royal lineage. Darnley, instead of our son, would then be back in the running as next in line for the throne in the event of my death."

By December 1566, Queen Mary and her court moved from Holyroodhouse to Stirling Castle, located some distance further west. The Baptism of Prince James was to be held there and, for this important occasion, the queen invited various celebrities including Queen Elizabeth of England and King Charles IX of France. Not surprisingly, these two notables did not appear at the event, but many Scottish nobles did attend. Prince James was baptized in December 1566 in the Royal Chapel of Stirling Castle.

"I thank you all for coming to this important event," she said to the guests. "Someday, James will rule as King of Scotland and I feel very confident about his destiny." Little did she realize that he would someday rule much more than Scotland.

After the baptism, Mary decided to travel to the estates of various nobles located some distance to the west. In her effort toward reconciliation with Darnley, she invited him to accompany her.

"Henry, would you be kind enough to accompany us on this journey? We will be traveling near your father's estate, and I am sure he would appreciate a visit from you and me."

"I guess I can go, although I hope it will not involve a very long period of time," he replied. There was little enthusiasm on his part, but Mary and others were looking forward to an interesting series of visits. The group proceeded toward the west.

A week later, Mary celebrated her twenty fifth birthday while on the tour. Near Glasgow, Darnley fell ill and was taken to his father's Castle, Lennox. The king's servants and others at Lennox took care of him. Leaving Darnley at Lennox, the queen returned to Holyroodhouse with her son.

"I should tell you," Lord Lennox said to his son after a few days of rest there, "that a number of threats to your security have come to us from the surrounding area. As soon as you are well enough to travel, I suggest that you return to Edinburgh as inconspicuously as possible."

Taking the advice of his father, Darnley did not stay long at Lennox Castle although still suffering somewhat from an infection. When he arrived in Edinburgh, it was considered unwise for him to go to Holyroodhouse because of a fear of spreading the infection to others there.

"I will stay in a private house at Kirk o' Field, not far from the palace," he said.

When Darnley was settled in the house, Bothwell, Huntley, Argyll and some others who disliked the king intensely saw their opportunity to get rid of him. "Let's agree on a plan to do away with the hated king for the good of Scotland," suggested Huntley boldly.

"Now that we know where he is spending the night, we can place some dynamite near his room and finish him off," said Argyll.

"The opportunity seems perfect," Huntly opined. "Lord Darnley will be recuperating at the house in Kirk o' Field and there will be little protection for him."

Bothwell, who hated Darnley as much as anyone, was glad to join the conspirators. Once Darnley was alone in bed in his room, Bothwell obtained the house keys, entered and placed gunpowder in the cellar. He lit the fuse and hurriedly left the house. Shortly thereafter, a loud blast was heard by many people in the area. A quick check of the scene by the conspirators indicated that the blast did not appear to harm Darnley at all. Disappointed with the results of the blast, Bothwell hurried away and returned to Holyroodhouse.

Although the blast did not kill him, Darnley became so frightened that, some minutes later, he bolted from the house. Friends of Bothwell saw Darnley and chased the king around the surrounding area. In the darkness, they grabbed Darnley and strangled him on the spot, leaving his body for others to discover. Then all of them rushed away from the scene of the crime.

The loud noise of the explosion alerted many people nearby and soon word reached the queen that Darnley had been murdered.

"Oh no, not another murder!" she cried. "How did it happen? Who did this horrible murder?" She was extremely disturbed by this death. She immediately got in touch with Bothwell who, she thought, was the logical person to help investigate the crime.

"Collect a group of soldiers and go immediately to Kirk o' Fields where the murder occurred. Search the area for evidence concerning the death of the king," she ordered.

"Yes, your highness. I will do as you order." Bothwell went to the garrison to gather a force of soldiers. While he had been part of the conspiracy, and had even lit the fuse for the explosion, he had left the house immediately. Someone else had actually murdered the king as he ran from the house.

In the meantime, nobles friendly to Bothwell and Huntley were on the alert.

Enemies of Bothwell and his friends strongly suspected that the chief suspect in the crime was none other than Bothwell himself. They accused him of the murder and made strong demands for his arrest. Lord Lennox, father of the late Lord Darnley, came immediately to Edinburgh.

"I demand vengeance for the death of my son," he proclaimed loudly.

He went to the queen and protested, "I ask your highness to support me in a request before parliament that Bothwell be charged with the murder of my son." He received considerable support from various nobles who disliked Bothwell. Under extreme pressure, Queen Mary allowed Lennox to bring action against Bothwell in front of the parliament accusing Bothwell of the slaying. Because of the presence of Bothwell's many supporters in the palace at the time, however, Lennox feared for his life and did not appear in parliament to plead his case. Consequently, the Lennox challenge fell flat.

Bothwell felt his defensive position now was very strong. He had about four thousand supporters in Edinburgh. But the opposition was strong and growing too.

"I am an honorable man," he bragged about the town, "and I am willing to defend my honor by dueling anyone who questions my honor." No one responded to the challenge.

The following week, the queen rode to Parliament with Bothwell carrying the scepter, the important symbol of royal power.

"Look at that," said one of the nobles, "Bothwell carries the scepter. There is no doubt now that he is the queen's right hand. He has achieved a position of great power and authority in Scotland."

Over a period of less than a year and a half, Bothwell had risen from a man banished from Scotland and living abroad to a powerful position as Queen Mary's strongest supporter. This remarkable rise in status had been achieved in the midst of bitter struggles between clans and factions in Scotland.

"Why do we see so little of Lady Jean, Bothwell's wife?" asked a nobleman in the parliament. "He seems all over the place while she is seldom seen with him."

"Bothwell's marriage to Lady Jean was no doubt a marriage of convenience for the ambitious nobleman. The wily earl greatly augmented his financial resources through that marriage. Now with his close relationship to the queen, he probably has access to all the wealth and power he wants. I doubt that he cares much for Lady Jean."

"And don't forget," his colleague commented, "Bothwell also had a mistress for several years, Anna Trondson, who finally departed Scotland and settled in Norway. I understand she was very bitter when he married Lady Jean, after years of promises to marry her. They even had a son together. And there were other mistresses. What I hear is that Bothwell has been sneaking off with the comely Bessie Crawford lately."

"I am still appalled by the murder of my husband," Queen Mary said to one of her maids weeks after the terrible event. I cannot get the horrible deed off my mind. I cannot concentrate."

"The king's death was horrible," the maid replied sympathetically, "but it cannot be changed."

Mary had difficulty adjusting to the new reality. Even though the king was of little help to her, she felt weak and inadequate in the face of Darnley's death. She also feared for her own safety now. To whom could she turn for strong support in bringing about reconciliation of the conflicting nobles, some of whom were pleased to see the king gone and others determined to punish the murderers? In these contentious circumstances she turned increasingly to Bothwell.

"I want to see the perpetrators of this crime punished," she told him, "but I must also bring about some reconciliation of contesting nobles. It seems nearly impossible. Tempers among them are at fever pitch. What should I do?"

"Finding the murderers is far less important right now than consolidating the power of the throne," he responded. Bothwell, of course, had no interest in finding the murderers. "We must maintain the strength of the central authority and defeat any attempt to compromise it. I'll do all I can to help your highness."

"It is evident that I am unable to reason with some of my opponents," she replied. "Perhaps you are right that we should put up a strong front against those seeking to undermine the throne."

Bothwell demonstrated a new aggressiveness in his dealings with the queen and also with her supporters and opponents.

Parliament, now dominated by Bothwell, granted lands to nobles favored by the new strong man of Scotland. In making such grants he obtained their commitment of political support, thus further strengthening his position in the Government. Those nobles who were denied royal favors were, of course, embittered and sought ways to undermine Bothwell politically.

Outwardly, the palace was in deep and lengthy mourning for Darnley, hiding the fear and anxiety felt by the queen. The extended mourning also masked the irrepressible determination of Bothwell to exercise power in the government and overcome his enemies among the nobles. In reaction, his opponents sought to join together and present a united front against him.

By March 1567, Bothwell was not only a powerful force in the government but also had moved into the palace, abandoning his wife, Lady Jean, who then initiated divorce proceedings against him. He did not contest her charges. She had served his purposes and now he was moving on to better things.

The dominant position of Bothwell in the government was now such that the queen could not resist his advances even if she wanted to do so. At this point, she probably was so dependent on him that she was quite willing to live with him. Bothwell's friends and supporters not surprisingly urged the queen to accept him as her close advisor.

Bothwell's opponents believed him guilty of the Darnley murder and attempted to bring the leading nobleman to trial. When the trial was set to begin, Bothwell surrounded the court with such a show of force that his accusers failed to appear. Bothwell produced a document supposedly proving his innocence. The court failed to convict Bothwell.

Significantly, this document also stated that the queen was "now destitute of a husband in which solitary state the commonwealth should not permit her to remain." The document noted that a native-born subject was to be preferred to a foreign prince. Several noblemen signed the document which was clearly designed to pave the way for Bothwell to marry the queen. Anyone refusing to sign the document was condemned and considered unworthy and a traitor. In view of this agreement, the queen clearly now could allow Bothwell to live in the palace.

One day in April, Bothwell warned the queen, saying "My intelligence indicates that opposition nobles are determined to seize you at the Holyroodhouse Palace. You are in great danger remaining in Edinburgh."

"But why?" she asked. "What is their intent?"

"That is not altogether clear," he replied. "They probably mean to force you to bend your policies toward their interests. Perhaps they mean to replace you. I'll not let that happen."

"What should we do?" she asked.

"I want you to ride with me and our loyalist forces to the Borders area where I can best protect you from your enemies."

In view of the threats Bothwell cited, she agreed to do as he proposed. As inconspicuously as possible, Mary and Bothwell left the palace and rode, with a sizable contingent of loyalist armed forces, into the Borders area. They went to Bothwell's Dunbar Castle on the coast and spent the night. In the meantime, baby James was held in Stirling Castle, the traditional nursery for Scottish princes, which was controlled by the queen's enemies, the Protestant opposition.

Although Bothwell had lived for some weeks in the Holyroodhouse palace, it was not clear to the general public whether they occupied the same bedroom or separate bedrooms. Bothwell intended that their stay together at Dunbar castle would make it clear that the two of them were living together virtually as man and wife. He wanted to place her in a position from which she could not avoid marrying him.

Whether or not she loved him or wished to marry him were matters now beside the point. He probably did not love her but saw distinct political advantage in a marriage to her. He had a strong motivation to solidify his position by marrying the queen and she was hardly in a position to object given his powerful position. She, too, probably considered marriage advantageous since his political and military support was apparently indispensable to her retaining the throne.

"Do you love me, James?" she asked when they were alone in the bedroom of Dunbar castle. For the past few weeks, she had been calling him James in private.

"Of course I do," he replied and kissed her as if to confirm his statement. Soon he went much further than merely a kiss.

"I look forward to our marriage, James. It will remove a cloud that has hung over us in the eyes of the people. Many have wondered about our relationship."

"I too will be glad when we marry and live clearly as man and wife."

"Before we marry, you will have to satisfy church authorities, both Catholic and Protestant, that you are no longer married to Lady Jean." Mary raised the troubling question.

"That should not be a problem. Lady Jean has asked for a divorce on the basis of adultery, and I have not denied it. More important, I have sought annulment of our marriage on the basis that Jean and I were too closely related, and officials of the Protestant church have declared the marriage null and void."

"That is good. I had a problem in that the Catholic church would not allow me to marry a divorced man," she said, "but if your marriage is null and void there would be no barrier imposed by Catholic officials to our marriage."

After a brief stay in Dunbar Castle, Bothwell, Queen Mary and the military contingent returned to Edinburgh. Bothwell became satisfied that whatever the earlier threat of the queen's abduction, the situation was now changed and they could safely return to the Holyroodhouse.

A priority task for the queen and Bothwell was to clear the air so they could be married. The Catholic Archbishop agreed to annul Bothwell's marriage to Lady Jean. Thus within a period of several days during the month of May, Bothwell became a free man, free to marry the queen.

"James, I feel that I should now take the action which you suggested and elevate your status in the government prior to our marriage."

"You mean concerning the Orkney Islands?" he inquired.

"Yes, we'll have a little ceremony during tomorrow's session of parliament." With considerable flourish, she named him the "Duke of Orkney and Lord of the Shetlands."

Despite appearances, the queen did not take this action independently. She was subjected to strong pressure for the appointment from the ambitious earl. He was pleased having the new position, once held by one of his ancestors.

Soon thereafter, on May 15, 1567, the twenty-five-year-old

Queen Mary and the thirty-two-year-old Earl of Bothwell were married in the Great Hall of Holyroodhouse Palace. The traditional year of mourning for the late king was ignored. The marriage ceremony was conducted according to the Protestant rite, indicating the dominance of Bothwell over the queen in palace affairs. Mary, a fervent Catholic, obviously made a major concession to Bothwell in agreeing to follow this Protestant rite.

Following the wedding, there was a formal dinner but no dancing as might have been expected after a royal wedding. Moreover, contrary to tradition, there were no rich presents for Bothwell and the queen from other heads of state, because of the brief period between sending invitations and the wedding itself. The entire atmosphere was formal and serious, with none of the merriment that generally accompanied an event of this kind.

Whatever her feelings for Bothwell, the queen could not have been very happy during this politically significant wedding. Memories of the murders of both Darnley and Ricco no doubt haunted her. In contrast, the ambitious Bothwell was probably elated since the event marked the culmination of his persistent struggle for dominance over the queen and the Scottish government. Although Mary had none of the warmth and temperament he demanded in a woman, he finally had achieved the pinnacle of power and influence as King of Scotland. The queen had the protection of a powerful and ambitious, if ruthless, man while he had the symbolic support of the royal head of state, useful to him in his own reach for power.

Following the marriage, the clouds of war gathered over Scotland. Many angry nobles opposed to Bothwell were seething with anger over the marriage and determined to destroy both royal heads of state. Among these opposition leaders was Kirkaldy, a leader of the old Protestant Party which was dominated by the queen's half brother, Lord James of Moray. Kirkaldy, Maitland and others hated Bothwell with great passion and plotted to take control of the government by force.

Anna Trondson, living in Bergen, Norway, learned from her highly placed relatives in the Norwegian Government that the

Earl of Bothwell had risen significantly in political power in the Scottish Government. This turn of events confirmed to Anna that his marriage to Lady Jean was motivated by ambitions for financial gain and political influence.

Little did Anna realize, at this stage, how far Bothwell had actually progressed in his rise to power. Events in Edinburgh had moved very fast indeed of late, including the earl's divorce from Lady Jean, the queen's appointment of the powerful Earl as Duke and especially his marriage to Queen Mary. Because these events had occurred in quick succession and news to the outside world traveled very slowly, Anna had not yet heard this latest dramatic news from Scotland.

Despite Anna's lack of knowledge of the most recent events, she knew enough about Bothwell to believe that the extremely ambitious admiral was capable of achieving such political power. She was also well aware that, in his struggle upward, he had been conniving and deceptive with others as well as her during those years of their close relationship. She realized now how glad she was to be rid of him!

"Have you heard what happened to your brother Enno?" Karen asked her daughter, Anna, one day in early 1567, some months after her arrival from Scotland.

"No. What happened to that restless brother of mine?"

"He and his cousin, Johannes Galtung, went to Sweden and became friendly with King Erik XIV and members of his royal family. You know Enno has been bitterly critical of the Danish King Frederick, your father's friend, for not restoring nobleman status to the so-called 'old nobility' of Norway," their mother explained "Even though Denmark and Norway are at war with Sweden, Enno went to Stockholm to seek the support of King Erik in pressing Norway to restore nobleman status to Norway's 'old nobility.' If that were done, Enno would be a recognized Norwegian nobleman because his ancestors were of a noble family. That is his goal."

"But how could Enno be so disloyal to King Frederick after all the king has done for our family?" Anna was exasperated.

"He is single-minded in seeking nobleman status," Karen replied. "He has taken a huge risk by being disloyal to King Frederick, and I am worried. Furthermore, he involved his cousin by asking him to return to Bergen and make a plea directly to officials here for the change of the nobility policy in Norway. Now, Johannes is confined to the Tower of Bergenhus and could be in danger of losing his life for disloyalty. I feel obliged to help Johannes if we can. He is so young and naïve."

"I'll go and see my cousin Erik Rosenkrantz, Governor General, and see if I can convince him that Johannes was innocently involved in this scheme of Enno's," Anna said.

"Oh, that would be a wonderful thing to do," replied her mother. "Johannes is such a fine young man."

"I'll go to see Erik tomorrow. Is there anything more about Enno that I should know?" Anna asked.

"Yes," Karen replied hesitantly, "It seems that a major theft occurred at the treasury of Gripsholm castle in Sweden while he was there and Enno is accused. Before he could be apprehended, however, he left Sweden and made his way to Germany."

"Goodness, what a mess he has made of things."

"You must try to help our dear cousin, Anna." Karen was very worried not only about Johannes but also Enno.

The following day, Anna met with cousin Erik who listened carefully to the story concerning the young man. "I believe you are right, Anna, Johannes Galtung was probably naïve and dominated by Enno. Under the circumstances, I think I can arrange that Johannes be released with the payment of a small fine."

"Thank you so much Erik. "This family appreciates your understanding and kindness." Anna would have reason to appreciate Erik's help in another way a few months later.

The following year, Anna and her mother learned that Enno committed murder in connection with a robbery in Germany, was found guilty and hanged. Although they mourned his death they could not justify his actions.

In Scotland by early June 1567, Bothwell and Mary's opponents had gained much strength. Bothwell determined that their personal safety required that they leave Holyroodhouse Palace and find a safer place for a time. "I underestimated the extent of the opposition that developed following our marriage," he admitted to her.

"Where would we go?" she asked. "How long a time do you think we should plan to be away?" Her heavy dependence on him was apparent.

"We should plan to be away for an extended period of time, say two months. If we can return to the palace sooner, all the better, but we should prepare for the longer period. I'll gather a sizable force of soldiers to accompany us." He started to leave the room.

"But you have not said where we will go." Mary cried.

"We will go to Borthwick Castle in the Borders. If they follow us, as I expect they will, we would have a good defensive position there." He hurried away to collect his soldiers.

Mary worried and reflected on their recent tumultuous days. After all these efforts to consolidate power, we have come to this. Now, all we can do is seek a good defensive position in the Borders and gain some time so that we might later overcome the opposition forces with the aid of the loyal soldiers still available.

On the fifteenth of June, Bothwell and Mary, with a contingent of loyal forces, fled Edinburgh and headed south. They stopped at Borthwick Castle, about six miles from the capital. Although their soldiers represented a sizable group of loyal forces, the opposition soldiers also were large in number and they pursued the royal couple with vigor and determination, finally stationing themselves around Borthwick Castle. A fight began between the opposing soldiers.

After a time, realizing the great strength of the rebels, Bothwell said to Mary, "I think it best if you leave the area, as I doubt we can defeat the rebels. I will follow later."

"But how can I possibly leave when we are surrounded by the enemy?" she cried.

"The rebels do not completely surround us, and I know a way out of here. Come and I'll show you. First, change your dress to that of a man to disguise your identity. Then when you are ready, leave by this pathway."

"While our soldiers and I continue the fight," he continued, "you can escape. We will meet later at Cakemuir Castle. Use this map to find your way." He handed her a rough map of the area. She did as she was told, obtaining men's clothes from the castle wardroom and departed through the route pointed out to her.

Bothwell and his men continued the fight, but the situation deteriorated indicating that it was time for him to leave. Having detailed knowledge of the castle and the surrounding area, Bothwell departed into the adjacent wooded and hilly area.

Within several hours Bothwell and Mary met at the rendezvous of Cakemuir Castle and continued their flight together from there. They knew that their pursuers in time would learn of their escape and follow them.

Mary and the new king, riding fast horses, headed eastward and finally stopped at Dunbar Castle on the coast. Since this castle was widely known to belong to Bothwell, the opposition leaders anticipated that the queen and Bothwell would probably go to this place. Before long, Bothwell's agents reported that a part of the pursuing force was indeed on the way to Dunbar. The royal couple knew they had to move on Their forces were outnumbered. They decided the best course of action was to return to Edinburgh and try to raise a sizable army in the capital city as quickly as possible.

Bothwell and Mary accompanied by a relatively small contingent of soldiers rode westward along the coast of the Firth of Forth toward Edinburgh and reached Seton Castle, only a few miles east of Edinburgh. Here they spent the night together. The opposition soldiers were able to trace the route of the royal couple and, on the following day, they surrounded Bothwell and Mary as well as their loyalist forces at Carberry Hill near Seton Castle.

At Carberry Hill, there was a standoff of the well-armed opposing forces, the leaders of each side somewhat uncertain how to proceed. Meanwhile many of the royal troops melted away as they saw the much greater strength of the opposition forces and foresaw their own defeat if they remained loyal to the throne. In the course of time, the two sides agreed to parley rather than fight.

The bargaining position of Bothwell and the queen was clearly very weak and becoming weaker as many of their military supporters abandoned them. Early in the negotiations, the opposition proposed that the queen leave Bothwell, saying they would then immediately acknowledge her as their sovereign. Mary refused, not trusting that opposition leaders would treat her with respect.

But as the royal supporters continued to drift to the other side, she relented and finally agreed to surrender herself to the Confederate Lords, the leaders of the opposition. She knew that a battle to resolve the matter would result in the defeat of her forces. Also, it seemed clear that unless they accepted the surrender terms, they would probably both be killed.

Under the terms of the agreement ultimately reached, Bothwell was to leave Carberry Hill with some of his supporters while the queen was to go over to the Confederate Lords. Bothwell would thus be allowed to go free. After completing this agreement, the royal couple embraced in full view of all.

"Goodbye, Mary," Bothwell said, "We are forced apart, but I wish you well with the Confederate Lords."

"Goodbye, James. Take care of yourself. Perhaps we will meet again under better circumstances."

"That seems doubtful." He let her go.

Then Bothwell and a few men quickly rode away from the area while Queen Mary surrendered to the rebel forces. The defeated king rode toward the Borders, the area he knew so well. He realized that his opponents would still pursue him at the earliest opportunity.

"Your highness, please come with us," said Kirkaldy. "We shall treat you well, but I can't say the same about Bothwell when we catch up with him, and we surely will."

"I expect you to treat me as the queen that I am, and I would consider it appropriate to treat the king with respect as well."

The cluster of opposition nobles took custody of the queen. She hoped she could trust them. She was taken to Craigmillur

Castle in Edinburgh rather than to Holyroodhouse. She was held there only briefly, however, as it was deemed too dangerous to keep her in Edinburgh given all the tension in the country. In particular, the Lords feared that, in the capital, Mary might attract enough supporters to regain political control once again.

Kirkaldy said to Lord James, "We have no intention of simply restoring her to the palace and allowing her to lead the government of Scotland as before her marriage to Bothwell."

"I should think not," said Lord James, "after all the trouble she has caused us. We will have to decide later, after discussions among us, what to do with her."

They were agreed, however, on the immediate disposition of the queen. She was taken by a group of nobles and soldiers across the Firth of Forth and then northward several miles to a small lake called Loch Leven. There she was transported in a boat to the Loch Leven Castle on the small island located near the center of the lake. This was the castle owned by Lord William Douglas.

Douglas was to be the queen's custodian, or jailer, while the Confederate Lords deliberated on their next course of action concerning Mary. She soon realized that her opponents had no intention of restoring her as the sovereign.

The Confederate Lords determined that this island castle would be Mary's prison at least until a decision could be reached as to what should ultimately be done with her. She spent about a year in the castle, carefully guarded to prevent her escape or communication with anyone outside the small island. Her captors knew very well that, around Scotland, she still had many supporters and some of them might try to restore her to the palace. The Confederates held the view that her escape from the Loch Leven Castle had to be prevented at all costs.

When Mary was taken to her island prison in Scotland, Anna Trondson was still living in western Norway. She was looking after her mother who was not well. In the summer of 1567, Anna had not yet heard the news of the marriage of Bothwell to Mary, nor did she hear about the later dramatic defeat of Bothwell and Queen Mary at Carberry Hill. So far as she knew, Bothwell was only an influential aide to Queen Mary. The Norwegian woman had little sympathy for Queen Mary, who had so unwisely chosen to give the ambitious Bothwell increasingly important positions in her government.

Queen Mary's child, James, was not allowed to be with her on Loch Leven island. He was held in the care of others at Stirling Castle, and she was not even permitted to see him.

At the time of Mary's surrender at Carberry Hill, the queen was again pregnant. In July 1567, she miscarried twins. Clearly, the father was Bothwell. The miscarriage avoided a further complication concerning succession to the throne of Scotland.

The same month that Mary miscarried the twins that she and Bothwell might have had, certain nobles came to her one day and demanded that she sign a statement abdicating her throne in favor of her son James. At first, she refused to sign the statement but, under strong pressure, she ultimately agreed to do so. Within days of that agreement, on July 29, 1567, Prince James, was crowned and declared King of Scotland as James VI. Lord Moray, Mary's half brother, was named regent for the young king who was then only 13 months old.

Lord Moray, who had been in exile in England, returned to Scotland. Finally, he was in the powerful position he had sought for so long. He paid a visit to Mary. The meeting was contentious, but she reluctantly had to agree to his becoming Regent for James VI.

Many months later, in May 1568, Mary discussed a possible escape from the island with George Douglas, an orphaned relative of Lord Douglas, the castle owner. George proved to be a willing conspirator and he enlisted the help of Willy Douglas, another orphaned relative of Lord Douglas. Together with Mary, George and Willie devised a plot for Mary's escape from the island.

Willy Douglas obtained the keys to the main gate of the castle and then, using a small boat, transported Mary, disguised as a maid, from the island to the shore. Here they were met by George Douglas and others who had horses. Mary was taken to the castle of Lord Seton, one of her loyal supporters.

After word of her escape became known around the area, many of those who were loyal to the former queen rushed to her aid. Mary offered to negotiate her position with Lord Moray but he refused. Soon two opposing forces were again ready for battle over the control of the government of Scotland. Mary's forces were greatly outnumbered and soon were forced to retreat toward Dumbarton near Glasgow.

Her hope was that at Dumbarton, her supporters could hold out against the opposition long enough for aid to be obtained from French forces. Aid from France, however, could only arrive after a considerable period of time and time was now critical. Before Mary and her armed force could even reach Dumbarton, a ferocious battle was fought in which Lord Moray's soldiers won a clear victory.

Mary and her depleted loyalists then retreated southward toward Dumfries with rebel forces in hot pursuit. Travel through this wild, rough country was difficult and there was little opportunity for rest along the way. It was clear that Mary's men could not overcome the much larger forces of her pursuers. Thus they continued to retreat.

Consideration was given to the possibility of her escaping to France where she would undoubtedly receive great sympathy and support. But there was no time to make the necessary arrangements for a ship to take her to France.

At Terregles, Mary made a momentous decision to escape to England and ask for refuge from English authorities. No doubt she realized that there was considerable danger in entering England, given the political background, but she also knew the danger of remaining in Scotland.

Mary reflected on the fact that Queen Elizabeth and many British people regarded her as a major threat to Elizabeth's position as Queen of England. The threat was exacerbated by the fact that Mary was a Catholic and would be entering a country that was strongly Protestant.

The alternative to entering England, however, was also extremely dangerous. There was a virtual certainly that she would soon be captured if she remained in Scotland. In that event, and in view of her recent confrontations with her Scottish enemies, she would probably be executed. The fact that she had abdicated her throne made it more likely that she would lose her life at the hands of her enraged enemies in Scotland.

Before she ventured into England, her friend and supporter, Lord Herries, wrote to the deputy governor of Carlisle, England, requesting permission for Mary to enter the area. He told the English authorities that Scottish enemies of the former head of state were closing in on her and, fearing capture, she wanted to enter England.

Permission to allow this controversial figure into England was not a matter to be taken lightly by local authorities. The local governor felt the need to make inquiries in London as to a course of action concerning such an important issue. These contacts and deliberations, of course, took precious time.

Without waiting for an answer to her request to enter the country, Mary crossed into the neighboring country. Boarding a fishing boat, she crossed the Solway Firth and soon arrived in Carlisle. She was installed in semi-captivity in Carlisle Castle. The local governor was not certain whether to treat Mary as a queen or a captive but, in any case, he was very cautious knowing that he had an extremely controversial figure in his area.

Before deciding on the disposition of the controversial Scottish figure, the governor insisted on consulting with Queen Elizabeth as to what action she wished him to take regarding this famous person. These inquiries and the deliberations in London were time consuming.

The presence of Mary in England represented a serious problem for Queen Elizabeth. Only a few years earlier, Mary had claimed to be the rightful Queen of England! Various solutions to the problem of what to do with her were considered by Elizabeth and her aides. They were in no hurry, however, to decide the question.

Months passed while the former Queen of Scots remained at Carlisle Castle. The following winter she was transferred to a more secure, but much less comfortable, prison at Tutbury in Stratfordshire. It became clear to Mary that she was not a guest of the English but a prisoner. Would her husband, the Earl of Bothwell, ever see her again?

After Bothwell said farewell to Queen Mary at Carberry Hill and was allowed to leave the area, he rode toward the east. Before long he arrived with his supporters at Dunbar Castle on the coast. Here he stayed a few days fully expecting his enemies to pursue him again in the near future. Fortunately for Bothwell, the Lords of Confederation were preoccupied with decisions concerning the disposition of Mary. Their primary interest was Mary and her child, James, the heir to the throne.

"I am quite worried," Bothwell said to his aide, French Paris, "that certain documents still at Holyroodhouse castle may fall into the hands of my enemies. These papers could prove embarrassing to me. You and another man must go to the castle and find those papers. Try to be as inconspicuous as possible in your entry to the palace and in your search for the documents. Here is a list of the papers I want and the places where they are filed."

"I'll find my partner and we will go immediately," the aide replied as he took the list and glanced at it. "The Lords of Confederation are elsewhere so we should have no trouble. The servants know us well so they will not be concerned."

"Good. Bring me the documents as soon as you can."

The Earl of Bothwell was deeply concerned that these documents, if they fell into the hands of the Lords of Confederation, could cause him a great deal of trouble by revealing his role in certain acts.

The two men successfully obtained the documents from the palace but as they were returning to Dunbar, they were intercepted by Moray's soldiers. The papers carried by one of the men were seized and carefully examined by Moray's supporters. The other man, French Paris, was able to elude Moray's soldiers and return to Dunbar with the rest of the papers in his possession.

Moray claimed that the papers taken from the Bothwell messenger contained evidence that Bothwell was the murderer of Darnley. A proclamation was immediately issued charging Bothwell with Darnley's death. Bothwell was ordered to appear at the

Tollbooth court in Edinburgh in two days time to answer the charges. Realizing that he now had only a relatively small number of supporters, Bothwell did not appear in the court. After this refusal, he knew that Moray and his forces would pursue him relentlessly.

"We'll leave Dunbar in two ships," Bothwell told his assembled men, a collection of about two hundred soldiers and sailors loyal to him. "Load the necessary provisions of arms, gunpowder, food and water in the ships and prepare to depart as soon as possible."

The men hurried to load the ships as ordered. Within a couple of hours, they raised the sails, shoved off from the pier and headed northward.

They first sailed to Spynie Castle in north Scotland to visit Bothwell's grand uncle and old tutor, the Bishop at Spynie. The bishop gave the admiral and his men shelter for the night. Refreshed the next morning, Admiral Bothwell and his men continued their journey toward the Orkney Islands. Bothwell was confident that Lord Moray, Leader of the Confederation, was pursuing him vigorously.

En route, the escaping Scots came across a heavily laden ship known to belong to Lord Moray. It seemed to be carrying mostly foodstuffs.

"Let's pull alongside the ship and see what we can find," Admiral Bothwell said to his men, "If it appears that they have food on board, we can increase our own provisions. We do not know how long we will be at sea. The ship seems to be unarmed."

No resistance was encountered. After taking large supplies of foodstuffs onboard, Bothwell's ships sailed to the Orkney Islands in their two small ships. They attempted to go ashore at Kirkwall but were rebuffed by local officials who refused to let them enter. Lacking the capabilities to seize Kirkwall, Bothwell then continued northward to the Shetland Islands.

He and his two hundred men were well received in the Shetland Islands where his position as Duke was officially recognized by local authorities. The Duke and his men were treated with great hospitality. Bothwell was also able to acquire some additional crew in the Shetland Islands.

"Men, I realize that Moray's forces are in hot pursuit of us," Bothwell said to his followers," so we cannot settle here comfortably now. Later, I feel sure we can return and settle in the islands. I feel sure Moray has a sizable number of ships under his command and we too should increase the size of our own fleet so we can deal with him effectively."

"But how can we do that in our present circumstances?" his aide questioned.

"Do you see those two merchant ships over there?" Bothwell asked. "They seem to have no defensive capability so let's take them. We can easily put the crews ashore."

Bothwell's ship immediately pulled alongside the Peliken, his men boarded it and took off the crew. Senior marine officers of Bothwell's group took over the captured German ship. Then the Scots went to the Breme, the other German merchant ship, and did the same. Now the escaping Scottish group had a fleet of four ships. All the men realized that they had now become pirates.

Lord Moray had four large, heavily-armed ships with four hundred men. They had left Leith port shortly after Bothwell's fleet departed Dunbar. Therefore they were not far behind the escaping forces. As Bothwell gathered additional crew and otherwise spent time in the Shetlands, Moray with his four ships pressed onward.

Moray surprised the Bothwell fleet and began a battle immediately. During the three-hour fight, two of Bothwell's ships were lost and two partly disabled. When stormy weather gathered, the pirate commander took advantage of the situation to flee northward with his two remaining somewhat disabled ships. Because of severe storms, Moray's fleet lost track of Bothwell's ships so the pirates escaped.

Many hours later, one of Bothwell's men reported that they were in sight of land but did not know the name of the place.

"It's the coast of Norway," the admiral said, "but I do not know the particular area. It is unfamiliar to me."

The small fleet approached the southwest coast of Norway. Here they saw a merchant ship. They pulled alongside the ship and Bothwell asked to speak with the master of the ship.

"We were caught in a severe storm last night and blown off course," he said to the master, "Could you tell us where we are located?"

"You are near Karmoi Sound. If you proceed toward that opening south of the island, you will reach a small port." Bothwell followed the suggestion and entered Karmoi Sound. Hardly had Bothwell anchored his two ships near the port than a Danish warship, the Bjornen, appeared in the sound.

Danish officers came aboard the lead ship and confronted Bothwell.

"Good morning, Sir," the Dane addressed Bothwell pleasantly. "You are in Norwegian waters, patrolled by the Danish-Norwegian Navy, and we would like to make a routine inspection of your papers."

"We have just been through a severe storm and most of our papers seem to have been lost in the confusion," Bothwell replied. He showed the Dane some papers concerning one of the ships but not the other.

"Since your papers are not in good order, I shall have to escort you to our Bergen naval headquarters for investigation." the Dane decided. You will please follow me to Bergen."

Bothwell protested, but to no avail.

As a result of this unexpected encounter, Bothwell and his vessels, including one hundred forty men, were brought to Bergen. He was permitted to take up residence in a hotel in the city until the Government received further orders from Danish naval officials. At this point, Danish and Norwegian officials were not aware of Bothwell's pirate operations in the vicinity of Orkney and the Shetland Islands. Initially, the Scotsman was regarded as a distinguished visitor and was entertained by Anna's cousin, Eric Rosenkrantz, who was the Danish King's top representative in Norway. Would Bergen officials discover the recent deeds of Bothwell and his fellow pirates?

CHAPTER 11

Anna Confronts The Admiral in Court

In September 1567, when Bothwell was brought to Bergen, Norway, Anna Trondson was living in the city with her mother, Karen. Karen had returned to her native Norway following the death of her husband in Copenhagen in 1565. The lonely widow was delighted to have Anna living with her. They had now been together in Bergen over a year.

The daughter and widow of the respected Admiral Kristoffer Trondson were able to have a life of leisure in an comfortable home in Bergen. They were members of the elite of the city which was the administrative center of the Norwegian Government, then a part of the Kingdom of Denmark and Norway. They attended many social affairs among the leading citizens of Bergen. In addition, Since Karen had a large number of married children and many grandchildren, all living in western Norway, they enjoyed many family visits in the region.

One evening, Anna attended a party in Bergenhus, the official home of Governor Erik Rosenkrantz, King Frederick's Representative in Norway. The Governor was a cousin of Anna. In a conversation with Erik during the party, Anna learned that a well-known Scotsman had just arrived in Bergen. Since she knew many Scotsmen during the time of her residence in that country she was curious who it might be.

"What is his name? Perhaps I know him or know the name," she said.

"Bothwell," Erik said, "he is James Hepburn, Lord Admiral

and the Earl of Bothwell. I seem to recall that you told me one time you knew him in Scotland."

Anna was incredulous. She did not reply immediately, trying to organize her thoughts. She could not believe James would come to Bergen, given all the turmoil in Scotland.

"Why, yes I do know him," she finally responded. "What is the reason for his visit to Bergen?" she inquired.

"It seems that he and his subordinates were sailing together in two ships near the Norwegian coast. They entered Norwegian-controlled waters and were intercepted in the Karmoi Sound by a Danish warship. Danish officers stopped the Scottish ships to review their papers, a customary routine."

"Weren't the papers in good order?" she asked.

"The admiral's papers were found to be open to question, that is, they were not entirely in order," Erik continued. "In accordance with standard procedures, the Danish naval captain brought Bothwell and his ships to Bergen for clarification of their status. It does not appear to be a major issue and will no doubt be resolved shortly."

"I see. And have you met the admiral?" she asked.

"Yes, we met briefly yesterday. He told me he hoped to leave Bergen very soon, but my officials have not yet completed their routine inquiries. He seemed eager to be on his way."

At that point, the Governor was called away by his wife and he excused himself. He left Anna wondering why James Hepburn was sailing near the Norwegian coast. Surely he would want to be in Scotland during unsettled times. The last she heard, there was a severe struggle for power among the various clans and factions in that volatile society and, in such a period, Bothwell's absence from the scene would seem to be politically hazardous for him.

Anna still did not know anything about the recent dramatic political events in Scotland, particularly the marriage of Bothwell and Queen Mary and the events that took place at Carberry Hill. Anna assumed that Bothwell still held a comparatively high position in the Government of Queen Mary. She could not conceive of why he was sailing along the Norwegian coast.

Anna wanted to learn the reason for Bothwell's presence on this coast. She decided to inquire further into his status by asking other governmental authorities in Bergen. Her cousin Erik did not seem to have knowledge of the details. She noticed, however, that a Danish navy captain was attending the party so she went to him.

"Captain Erling, it is nice to see you again. I believe the Bjornon is your ship and that you recently arrived from the Karmoi area."

"Good evening, Miss Trondson. How nice to see you. Yes, you are correct about my ship."

"Governor Rosenkrantz told me a few minutes ago that you have detained a Scottish admiral. I understand that you are reviewing his status since his papers were open to some question. Is he still being detained?"

"Yes, we are not yet satisfied that his papers are in order. He has two ships and we are holding them as well."

"Do you expect to hold him much longer?"

"A few days more, I expect. Why are you interested in this man? Do you know him?" the captain inquired.

"I knew him quite well in Scotland but I have not seen him for more than a year. He was then a well placed man in the government of Queen Mary," Anna added. "but I do not regard him as a man of good character."

"That is an interesting observation. I shall keep that in mind."

"Thank you for the information," Anna said. "I look forward to learning about the disposition of the case."

"And I thank you for your statement about the admiral."

Anna moved along and tried to hide her perplexity as she held conversations with other friends. Meanwhile, she reflected on her conversation with the captain. He said Bothwell has two ships in Bergen and that they were being held pending disposition of the issue of the admiral's status.

She was still sorely bitter about the admiral's abominable treatment of her over a period of years. It occurred to Anna that James was no doubt a very rich and powerful man after marrying Lady Jean and becoming a leading figure in the Scottish Parliament. Therefore, he should certainly be in a position to make some amends for his mistreatment of her during the years she lost waiting for him to make good on his promises. Not even the arrival of their son persuaded him to marry her and raise a family. He was clearly a cold-hearted man and deserved to be compelled to face her and at least apologize for his misdeeds.

Why not also seek some compensation from him for his mistreatment of her? She decided that she would confront him in a Bergen court with certain financial demands. If he showed no compassion early in the proceedings, she would become more demanding.

Two days later, Bothwell was dumfounded to be summoned to a Bergen civil court to respond to the suit brought by Anna Trondson. Two days after receiving the summons, James appeared in the courtroom and completely ignored Anna, leaving the matter entirely to his attorney. A lawyer represented Anna so she did not have to talk with him directly.

Anna's suit against Bothwell sought damages for his mistreatment of her, and particularly for his false promises to marry her. Her lawyer stated to the court, "The admiral took the young Anna Trondson from the home of her parents in Copenhagen to Amsterdam, promising to marry her and then failed to do so. He left her in that city for an extended period of time without providing her sufficient money to support herself during his extended absence and, as a result, she had to sell her jewels to obtain funds. Furthermore she had lent him money and he never repaid it. She should be compensated for this poor treatment."

Bothwell felt great humiliation hearing all of this personal information related in the court. As to the merits of her case, his lawyer stated, "There is no truth to any of her charges against the admiral. They are fabrications of a woman seeking to gain compensation from this noble gentleman. She cannot prove any of these outrageous allegations. I move that the case brought by this irresponsible woman be dismissed."

Her lawyer then addressed the judge, "Your honor, we anticipated that the admiral would react in this way. Therefore, my client has brought to the court various letters which Miss

Trondson wrote to the admiral at various times during their courtship. In these letters she discusses in great detail numerous aspects of their relationship. These letters fully support her description of his treatment of her. Miss Trondson was able to recover these letters while she was living on his estate in Scotland. Moreover, she has supplied the court with informal notes in the admiral's own hand written to Miss Trondson at various times. These letters and notes completely confirm Miss Trondson's allegations."

The judge addressed the admiral and his lawyer, "Does the defendant wish to contest the contents of these letters?" Bothwell and his lawyer conferred a few minutes and then the lawyer replied, "No, your honor. We are willing to make a reasonable settlement with the plaintiff."

"What do you demand as compensation from the defendant?" the judge asked Miss. Trondson and her attorney.

They consulted about the issue briefly and then her lawyer stated, "My client would accept title to the smaller of the two ships he owns and a reasonable financial settlement."

Bothwell and his lawyer again conferred and then the latter addressed the judge, "The admiral agrees to turn over ownership of the smaller ship and also agrees to provide her with an annuity after he returns to Scotland where he will arrange it."

Anna was entirely satisfied with the settlement and the case was closed. She felt that she had achieved not only substantial compensation from her former fiance but, even more importantly, he was forced to admit in open court that he had treated her very badly. The latter gave Anna particular satisfaction.

As to the ship, she would dispose of it as soon as possible for whatever price she could obtain. The promised annuity, she knew, would probably never materialize. She had learned more about the situation in Scotland since his arrival in Bergen . . . Who could know when he might return to Scotland and carry out the purpose of the Bergen court. In spite of the uncertainty, she was very pleased with the outcome of the trial.

Prior to his appearance in court, Bothwell was confident that the suit brought by Anna was a mere nuisance, and he wanted the contested issues of the case resolved as quickly as possible. He realized that his continued detention by the Danish-Norwegian government was far more threatening than Anna's court action. When he learned that Anna had incriminating evidence in the form of letters to support her charges, he wanted to settle the case at once at any price. He needed to focus on the vital detention issue.

Bothwell knew he had to conceal from the authorities his recent important role in the Scottish Government and particularly the various major charges, including murder, brought against him by Scottish officials now in charge of that government. The detained Scottish admiral concentrated his attention again on the basic issue of establishing, to the satisfaction of Danish and Norwegian authorities, that his papers were in sufficient order.

Earlier, on arrival in Bergen, naval authorities had hastily escorted him from his ship and he did not then have an opportunity to retrieve all of his private papers and take them with him. Now, Bothwell desperately wanted to obtain those papers and destroy them because they contained information that would show him to be culpable in certain serious offenses in Scotland.

"I have certain papers on my ship which I am sure will establish the good standing of my men and myself," the admiral said to the responsible Naval officer. "Please allow me to go aboard my ship and recover those papers."

"It will not be necessary for you to go aboard your ship. We will search for the documents ourselves," said the skeptical officer. He suspected that the admiral might be more interested in destroying evidence that securing information to support his case.

"But I can find the papers more readily," Bothwell persisted. "Just give me a short time on the ship and I will present them to you." He knew there was no other way he could secure those incriminating papers.

Not surprisingly, Bothwell's request to obtain the personal papers himself was firmly denied. Instead of allowing Bothwell to retrieve the papers himself, Norwegian officials boarded the ship and found them. They examined the documents carefully. Among the papers were official proclamations against Bothwell stating that he was a traitor to Scotland and guilty of murderer. A letter in the handwriting of the queen complained of the cruel fate that had fallen on both her and Bothwell.

After examining these documents, the Governor General decided that Bothwell was such a prominent figure of Scotland that it would be inappropriate for officials in Bergen to deal with him further. He did not disclose to the Scotsman the contents of the papers found on the ship but was sure Bothwell knew what they had found.

Governor Rosenkrantz directed that the admiral be sent immediately to Copenhagen on one of the King's naval ships. Bothwell was permitted to take with him no more than four of his men as aides. Aboard ship, the admiral was treated as a notable person with freedom of movement about the naval vessel.

When the warship arrived in Copenhagen, the king was out of the city. Acting officials provided the Scotsman good accommodations appropriate to his status as a nobleman. Nevertheless, he was kept under close watch by royal guards. The four aides who accompanied him on the voyage from Bergen were permitted to continue serving him. When King Frederick returned to Copenhagen, he reviewed the situation with his subordinates but did not wish to meet Bothwell personally. The king ordered that the admiral continue to be held.

Weeks later, Lord Moray, the Regent of Scotland requested that King Frederick return Admiral Bothwell to Scotland. The Danish king refused. Instead he gave instructions that the Scotsman was to be retained in a castle outside Copenhagen. Relocated, the admiral was housed in comfortable accommodations in a castle although he was not given freedom to leave the castle. King Frederick still refused to see him despite repeated requests from Bothwell for a meeting. The fact that the king and Bothwell had participated in many meetings together in 1560 was considered by the king as of no significance so far as the present case was concerned.

Bothwell was, of course, eager to plead his case for freedom. He wrote a letter to the Danish king indicating that when his ships were seized in Karmoi Sound he was actually on his way to Copenhagen to inform King Frederick of the wrongs committed by others against the Queen of Scots. Furthermore, he stated that he also intended to proceed to France and inform the King of France of the misdeeds against the queen of Scotland.

The king was not impressed with Bothwell's dubious explanations of his actions in the North Sea and around Norway. Frederick had various independent sources of information concerning the admiral indicating that what happened in Scotland was at odds with the Scotsman's story. The king also had a vague memory that Bothwell had wronged Admiral Trondson's daughter. He therefore ordered that the admiral be held indefinitely.

The king advised Lord Moray that he would not return Bothwell to Scotland but rather would hold him in close confinement. Frederick thought the detained admiral might be useful as a bargaining chip in his dealings with European governments, particularly with Scotland and his sometime enemy, England.

The status of Admiral Bothwell in Denmark and that of Queen Mary in England were somewhat similar in that both were treated initially as guests but, before long, they became aware that they were actually prisoners. When Bothwell first arrived in Copenhagen he was given fine accommodations in a castle and allowed to retain a number of personal servants. Similarly when the queen arrived in Carlisle, England, she was given fine accommodations and was permitted to have a number of servants to look after her every need. Over a period of months, however, both of these prominent persons found their status gradually change from respected visitor to that of well-guarded prisoners.

In the course of time, the conditions under which the admiral lived became more and more austere, and it was increasingly clear to Bothwell that he was indeed a prisoner. His servants were withdrawn and his quarters were reduced both in size and quality. He protested these unwelcome moves but to no avail.

Early in 1568, after some weeks in different locations in Copenhagen, Bothwell was taken to an apartment in the Malmo castle for better security. As he was transported by carriage from the port in Malmo to the nearby castle, he could not help reflecting on the time he and Anna Trondson visited the Malmo castle. They were then treated with great respect by the governor who gave them a tour of the castle and invited them to have tea. Now, he was taken to the castle as a prisoner, although the word "prisoner" was not used by the king or his subordinates. When settled in his apartment prison, Bothwell had much time to study and write during the long days and weeks of his detention.

One day he said to Sven Anderson, the official responsible for keeping him under close confinement, "I have just completed writing a document that explains fully the circumstances that led to my detention in Copenhagen, and this explanation of my activities prior to my being taken into custody clearly shows the reasons I should be released immediately and allowed to proceed to France where I prefer to relocate. I would appreciate your delivering a copy of my paper to King Frederick and providing a copy to the French ambassador to Denmark."

"What is the title of your paper?" Sven asked.

"Les Affaires du Compte de Boduel," the earl replied. "I have written it in French for the convenience of my readers. I know the king is fluent in French and can easily read it."

"Before accepting the document, the king will want to know the purpose of the paper," Sven responded, "How should I reply?" Sven sensed that the king would not want to waste valuable time reading a pointless paper by Bothwell. Nevertheless, Sven did not want to take the responsibility of refusing to deliver a document addressed to the king.

"My purpose," Bothwell replied, "is to present a full account of the facts leading up to my arrest. When the king and the ambassador see this detailed and accurate statement of the facts surrounding my case, they will see at once the injustice of my confinement. Accordingly, the king will agree to my release immediately, allowing me to go to France."

"So the purpose of the paper is basically to argue your case for release from confinement here," Sven said, using his own words to summarize the earl's objective.

"I prefer my own way of stating it," Bothwell replied.

"I'll deliver the papers as you request," Sven told him.

The paper did not result in his release nor any improvement in the conditions under which he was held. The king dismissed the document as a self-serving effort by Bothwell to present himself as innocent of any wrong-doing. The French ambassador did not feel he had sufficient independent knowledge of the circumstances of the case to judge the validity of Bothwell's assertions and therefore deferred to King Frederick on the matter.

As Bothwell sat in his Malmo room with much time on his hands, he considered every possible means of securing his release. After a time, he tried yet another tactic that he thought might prove appealing to King Frederick.

He wrote a letter to King Frederick in February 1568 offering him the islands of Orkney and Shetlands as recompense for his freedom. Orkney and the Shetlands had come under Bothwell's official responsibility when Queen Mary appointed him Duke of that island region in the previous year. Thus the offer had the appearance of a legitimate and generous proposal.

Unfortunately for the imprisoned admiral, official transfer of this territory to Denmark was almost certainly doomed because of Bothwell's dubious political standing in Scotland at the time. Lord James, long a bitter foe of Bothwell, was now in control of the Scottish Government. If Lord James could get hold of Bothwell he would undoubtedly have him executed. Much as King Frederick would like possession of the islands, he was certain that there was no way that their ownership could be transferred to Denmark. Consequently, the king was unimpressed by the offer and gave it no serious consideration. He gave Bothwell no formal response to the proposal. He simply ignored it.

Bothwell continued to be held in custody. In the meantime, Lord James Moray sent further requests to Denmark seeking release of the prisoner to him. Had the prisoner been sent to Scotland there is no doubt he would have been subject to a biased trial, torture and death. The Scottish government's requests were refused without explanations. Queen Elizabeth also requested that King Frederick release Bothwell to her government. That request, too, was denied by the king. It is quite uncertain what kind of treatment Bothwell would have received had Frederick turned the prisoner over to English authorities, but there is a good chance that he would have been severely punished for his depredations in the English territory bordering Scotland, an area where he was hated by the local population.

King Frederick believed he had a valuable pawn to play in an international game of chess, particularly since England was a major rival of Denmark in international affairs. He felt that that he could use the Scotsman to his advantage in his dealings with both England and Scotland.

King Frederick thought there was a chance, however remote, that Mary and Bothwell might someday rule England if both were freed from prison. The king knew Mary was a presumptive heir to the English throne and Bothwell was married to Mary Queen of Scots. Given that Frederick held Bothwell firmly under his control, he could potentially use his prisoner as a pawn, exerting strong influence over the future leadership of England.

In a different scenario, the king mused, if through some political bargaining in England, Mary were returned to Scotland as the sovereign queen and if she wanted Bothwell back in Edinburgh to take his former place as king, what might she be willing to offer King Frederick for his release? Interesting possibilities. He would hold the admiral and see what developed.

As months passed and the cause of the Queen of Scots in England became hopeless, Bothwell's value to Frederick as a bargaining chip declined markedly. He was treated less and less well by the Danish King. Accordingly, the quality of the prisoner's quarters was greatly reduced.

Finally, when the Scotsman's value to the king as a pawn in international politics was near zero, Bothwell was moved, in 1573, to the notorious Dragsholm prison located northwest of Copenhagen. Dragsholm, built in the 13th century, was one of the largest and strongest fortresses in Denmark. During the time of King Frederick, it was used as a prison for those members of the nobility whom the king wanted to push out of the way.

Dragsholm prison was far worse than the previous quarters Bothwell occupied in Copenhagen and elsewhere. In the latest facility, he was kept in solitary confinement in a very small cell. No visitors at all were allowed. His physical health declined. An old wound tracing back to his injury in the Borders of Scotland became troublesome and he suffered great pain as a result. It is said that he was in such pain that he tried to commit suicide by butting his head against the prison wall. This self-destructive behavior was halted by securing Bothwell with a short, heavy chain to a post in the center of the cell so that he could not reach the wall.

Five years after Bothwell was sent to Dragsholm, Queen Elizabeth sent one of Bothwell's personal enemies, John Clark, to Denmark with orders to bring the Scotsman back to the Tower of London on a charge of high treason. The queen told Clark that his own life would be sacrificed if he failed in this mission. He failed, of course, and was captured by the Danes. King Frederick put Clark in the same miserable prison with Bothwell.

Both Clark and Bothwell died in the Dragsholm prison during the same week of April 1578. For Clark, his imprisonment lasted only about a year, but no doubt it was a very painful imprisonment. Bothwell's incarceration at Dragshom lasted five long years and caused him to have a mental breakdown during the later stages of his imprisonment. It is hard to imagine the dreadful circumstances of the admiral's long confinement at Dragsholm.

Bothwell and Clark were buried near Feirvejle Church located in close proximity to the prison. Today, Bothwell's remains rest in a tomb inside that small, quaint church.

Mary Queen of Scots also had a terrible ending after a long period of confinement in various places in England. The conditions of her detention in various castles were far better than the horrendous Dragsholm prison cell where Bothwell was held. Yet she too was kept under close guard at all times to prevent her escape. The conditions of her confinement became progressively more harsh over the 20 years of her imprisonment in England.

The Scottish queen frequently pressed the English Government to release her but Queen Elizabeth was adamant. Mary secretly communicated with various influential individuals both inside and outside England in efforts to encourage them to rescue her but, unfortunately for Mary, these conspiracies were discovered by agents of Queen Elizabeth.

Finally, after two decades of imprisonment and then a brief trial, Mary Queen of Scots was found guilty of crimes and beheaded on February 8, 1587, in Fotheringham Castle near Nottingham, England. Queen Elizabeth could not tolerate the continued threat that Mary represented as a possible Queen of England. James, the son of Mary Queen of Scots, however, became not only James VI of Scotland but also succeeded Queen Elizabeth as King James I of England.

Bothwell and Mary Queen of Scots paid dearly for their misjudgments and reckless actions in Scotland. Although Scotland at that time was torn by clan rivalries and religious intolerance making the country difficult to govern, both these leaders demonstrated major faults and shortcomings that led to their downfall. Bothwell's unbridled ambition and Queen Mary's decision to rely on the unprincipled Bothwell were key factors in their ultimate defeat and the horrible death each suffered.

CHAPTER 12

Anna's Marriage in Norway

Anna matured a great deal during the several years following her departure from her Copenhagen home with the flamboyant Bothwell in the summer of 1560. Now with the punishing experience behind her, she was creating a new life in her native land of Norway. Here, she was near her mother and sisters, all of whom were more important to her now than ever before.

Karen and Kristoffer had a large family of seven daughters and a son. Most of the children were born in the Hardanger area of western Norway and spent their early years in that pleasant region.

Dortea remained particularly close to Anna. After her marriage to Lord John Stuart ended with his accidental death, she married again and settled on a farm in Norway. The Trondson"s daughter Else also married a Scotsman, the rich Anders Mowatt, and they settled in Tysnes, Norway. Anna's sister Margaret married a Danish nobleman, Jorgen Pederson Stauer, manager of the Sunnhordland District of western Norway. Anna's sister Kristine married Torbjorn Olavson Sandven, owner of a large estate in western Norway and, for a time, a sheriff. Two other sisters, Magdalena and Maren, also settled in western Norway.

The wide family circle provided Anna opportunity for many visits around western Norway, particularly in the Hardanger area where she had spent her own early childhood. Although she desperately missed her son, she felt comfortable here and firmly accepted. What Anna did miss in Norway was someone to love with whom she could spend the rest her life in a good marriage.

Else and her husband Anders were very fond of entertaining

friends and relatives in their fine home on a large estate in Seim, located along the Hardanger Fjord. One summer day, a large gathering of invitees celebrated the fifth wedding anniversary of their hosts. Among the guests were Anna and her mother, Karen. Also present were Governor Erik Rosenkrantz, and his wife Helvig. The governor brought with him a friend named Erik Hjone, a former captain in the Norwegian Navy. He had been injured some months earlier in the Seven Years War between Denmark and Sweden, a war that was still being fought in the late summer of 1567.

"Anna, may I introduce Captain Erik Hjone," Rosenkrantz said when the opportunity arose for the introduction.

"I am pleased to meet you," Captain Hjone said enthusiastically. "As a captain in the Norwegian Navy, I had the honor of serving under your father some years ago."

"It is a pleasure to meet someone who knew my father," Anna, replied. Then, turning to Rosenkrantz, she said, "Cousin Erik, you are most kind to introduce me to a naval officer who served under my dear father."

"As you can see, Anna, Captain Hjone lost an arm. It happened in a naval engagement with a Swedish ship. He also had the misfortune of losing his wife recently." He winked mischievously at Anna.

"I am sorry to hear of your misfortunes. You must be very proud of your service in the navy."

"Yes, the navy was my life. Now I have to begin a new career."

"Well, you are still a young man," she replied, guessing that he could not be more than 35 years of age. "What will you do now?" she inquired.

"I shall take over a farm in the Hardanger area from my father who now feels that he is too old to continue operating the farm and desires to move to Bergen."

"Would you like to take a walk in the garden?" he asked. She was agreeable and they continued their conversation in a long leisurely stroll around the estate.

Looking out the window of the house, Else saw the couple in

the distance and addressed her husband, Anders. "When I observed cousin Erik introducing this handsome guest to Anna, I had a feeling he was match-making."

"If so, he was serving a very good cause. Anna needs to find a husband."

"I agree," Else said, "but she is fearful of making another dreadful mistake. She is still haunted by her experience with Bothwell."

Anders was reflective. "I have noticed that she is very careful in evaluating eligible men she meets and has rejected more than a few possible mates who would gladly marry her."

"Let's hope she is not afraid to marry. I'm sure she'll make the right choice when the time comes."

During the course of the next few months, Erik and Anna spent considerable time together, both in Bergen and in the Hardanger area. She visited his estate and admired the diligence with which he tackled his new occupation. His relations with his farm helpers were excellent. The prospects for his success in this new venture seemed good. More importantly, she enjoyed being with him.

It was inevitable, of course, that he would learn something about Anna's affair with Bothwell. After all, the romance had lasted several years and had never been a secret. She was afraid to tell him very much about her life in those years for fear he would turn away from her, and she was already growing very fond of him. For his part, he was reluctant to press her for details, preferring that she volunteer information. At the same time, Erik felt he had to know more about her past life. He was very much in love and wanted to ask her to be his wife.

"I know you feel I have not been very forthcoming in telling you about recent years of my life," Anna began one evening when they were strolling along the harbor area of Bergen. "It is difficult for me to explain the affair with the flashy Scotsman, Bothwell, who for a considerable period of time seemed such a good man and promised to marry me. I thought I loved him and waited patiently for him. I waited in vain."

"I realize how difficult it must be for you to discuss this subject," he said sympathetically. "My only interest in the matter is to have assurance that the affair is over and that you have no regrets that it is ended."

"Oh it is definitely ended!" she replied with conviction.

"I am happy to hear you say that," Erik replied.

She was quiet a few moments, wondering what more there was to be said. Then she began again. "I was young at the time I met him, and I was very impressionable. Bothwell was very attentive to my desires and behaved like a gentleman. He was a dashing young admiral of apparent good standing and appeared to have a promising career."

Erik was tempted to ask her why she changed her opinion of him only after so many years had passed. But he restrained himself and waited for her to continue.

"I sensed, at times when I was alone, that he was not sincere in his promises. I thought of leaving many times. Then when we were together he seemed so glad to see me that my doubts vanished and I was smitten again. Also, after considerable time passed, I felt I had invested, so to speak, too much time in our relationship to provoke a confrontation over the issue of fixing a firm date for our marriage."

"What finally made you realize that he was not honest with you?" The question was more blunt than Erik intended, but now it was out there.

Anna did not reply immediately but took a moment to gather her thoughts. "Bothwell told me in February 1566 that he intended to marry Lady Jean Gordon. That statement, of course, confirmed my occasional suspicions. There was no more doubt about his love for me. He would never marry me. I am embarrassed and ashamed that it took me so long to realize that he had been deceiving me for so many years."

"I assume you left Scotland after hearing him make that statement," Erik said.

"I left the country at the first opportunity. In two weeks time I arrived in Bergen. I should also tell you that Bothwell and I had a child, William, and Bothwell did not allow me to take my son with me when I left Scotland. William has been well cared for by his grandmother, Lady Sinclair. She has allowed William to visit me from time to time in Norway. He is a fine boy. You would like him."

"I'm glad you and William have a good relationship. I would like to meet him."

"I expect him to visit again later this year."

"And what have been your thoughts about Bothwell since you arrived in Norway?"

"I have reflected on the man's character and came to realize that he is a man of unbridled ambition. I do not think he was ever capable of loving anyone. He married Lady Jean for political and financial gains, not for love. He later married Mary Queen of Scots to achieve political power and riches. He proved himself to be extremely clever in pursuing both power and wealth up to a point. I see myself as having been a victim of his driving ambitions."

"Then you have no feelings of regret about ending the relationship with Bothwell?"

"I only regret that the relationship did not end much sooner or, better still, had never begun."

"I am glad you told me this story. It reinforces my belief that you had an unfortunate experience and that you are now free to begin a new, more hopeful chapter in your life."

She was extremely relieved that he reacted so positively to her long and candid discourse on her misfortune. What a wonderful man to have such understanding and compassion, she thought.

Erik held her close and said softly, "I love you Anna! Will you marry me?"

Anna was overwhelmed: "Oh yes, Erik. I love you with all my heart. Nothing would make me happier than to marry you!"

A few weeks later in the Spring of 1568, a wedding was held in the ancient Kvinnherad Lutheran Church in Rosendal. After the marriage ceremony in the small church, a large wedding party was held at the Seim estate of Erik Hjone and Anna. Attending the party were many guests including Anna's mother, Anna's several sisters and their husbands, Erik's father, Governor Rosenkrantz, and many others. A splendid dinner was served, followed by dancing long into the night.

Erik and Anna settled on the Hardanger farm that Erik had inherited from his father. Anna often reflected on how fortunate she was in meeting a man she could trust and love without reservation.

In the first few years after their marriage, she found herself occasionally contemplating the kind of chaotic and unstable life she would likely have experienced had she married the duplicitous James Hepburn. As time passed she thought less about him.

She had heard, of course, that the Danish king held Bothwell in close confinement at Malmo castle from 1568 until 1573 when he was sent to Dragsholm prison. In Anna's view, the deceitful, reckless and ambitious Scotsman had surely earned imprisonment. Perhaps if she knew about the extremely harsh conditions under which he was held after 1573 she might have had a bit of pity for him. Since she knew no details concerning his prison circumstances, her feelings toward him during this critical time were not tested.

News of Bothwell's death in prison came to her late in 1578. By this time, she rarely thought about him. Life for her and Erik in Norway had become serene and happy. Two delightful children had been born to them. As to the past, the brief periods of time she spent with Bothwell in Copenhagen and Amsterdam and the five years she spent in Scotland waiting for James Hepburn to marry her were now but fading memories.

There was, however, a significant legacy of her years of association with James Hepburn, namely, their son William who remained in Scotland with his grandmother when Anna left Scotland in 1566. Lady Sinclair raised the boy well and encouraged him to correspond regularly with his mother. Anna was very appreciative of Lady Sinclair's kindness in fostering a good relationship between Anna and her son.

On a few occasions in recent years, William had traveled to Norway and spent enjoyable visits with Anna and her family. In 1578, the year that his father died in Dragsholm prison, the Fifth

Earl of Bothwell was sixteen years old and about to be sent, like his father before him, to France for further education. Every indication was that the young man had the potential to become a gentleman and an influential leader in Scotland. Anna hoped that he would become more honorable than his father, both in his pursuit of a career and his treatment of women, including in particular the woman he someday would profess to love.